I hate to be conspicuous. I get embarrassed very easily—like if my mother talks too loud to people in the supermarket. I have often thought how relaxing it would be to be invisible. But when I took over Richard's paper route and they said "girls can't deliver papers," I had to speak out. And then people called me a nut. A women's liberation nut! All I wanted was for things to be fair.

I used to think there was something sort of embarrassing about women's liberation. All those jokes about burning bras. The only bra I had was called Little Miss Beginner, which is the only kind that fits somebody my age, and I was certainly not going to burn it.

My book will not be the kind that tells "How Tomboy Mindy discovered that growing up gracefully can be as exciting as playing baseball." It will not be written in that way they call "bouncy and lighthearted" on book jackets. My book is going to tell about the ideas and adventures of the real me, Barbara Fisher. And it will be true.

The Real Me

The Real Me *by Betty Miles*

ALFRED A. KNOPF · NEW YORK

G560718

THIS IS A BORZOI BOOK
PUBLISHED BY ALFRED A. KNOPF, INC.

Copyright © 1974 by Betty Miles. All rights reserved under International and Pan-American Copyright Conventions. Published in the United States by Alfred A. Knopf, Inc., New York, and simultaneously in Canada by Random House of Canada Limited, Toronto. Distributed by Random House, Inc., New York.
Manufactured in the United States of America

Library of Congress Cataloging in Publication Data

Miles, Betty. The real me.
SUMMARY: An eleven-year-old girl tells about her efforts to end sex discrimination in choosing classes at school and her fight to have a paper route.
[1. Family life—Fiction. 2. Women's rights—Fiction] I. Title.
PZ7.M594Re [Fic] 74–160
ISBN 0-394-82838-0 ISBN 0-394-92838-5 (lib. bdg.)

for my family, especially Ellen.

The Real Me

INTRODUCTION

I THINK SOME of the old proverbs are wrong. For example, "You can't tell a book by its cover." I usually *can* tell a book by its cover. I read a lot of books, and I have noticed that the ones that turn out to be bad often have dumb cover pictures. The worst books, the ones that I do not even bother to take home from the library, all seem to have the very same sappy story on the inside of the cover. The story is: "How Tomboy Mindy, who loves to play baseball and climb trees with the boys, meets handsome Michael and discovers that growing up gracefully to be a young lady can be even more exciting."

Too bad on Tomboy Mindy, the dope.

My book is not going to tell about "growing up gracefully," that's for sure. And I will not write it in that way they call "bouncy" or "lighthearted" on the cover. My book will tell about the real life of me, Barbara Fisher. And it will be true.

In grade school, we always had to write about My

Summer Vacation, or My Life. We were supposed to say things like:

My name is Barbara Fisher. I am eleven years old. I live with my mother and father and my brother Richard in Fair Park, New York. My favorite animal is The Dog. My favorite color is blue.

Actually, my favorite color is not blue. I love bright colors like red and purple, and dry colors like beige and brown, and silky colors like ivory. But it is too complicated to say all that, so I just used to put blue. That is the difference between writing in grade school and being a writer. A writer tries to tell the truth, even when it is complicated.

I can see already that it is not easy to write a book, especially if, like me, you have a lot to say. But I have been writing essays about my ideas all this year, so I am used to thinking about how I feel, and writing it down. My English teacher, Miss Peretti, says, "Essays are revealing of one's personal point of view, which is different from anyone else's." You will see what my personal point of view is on many topics, because I am going to put some of my essays in this book. The first one will be "On Books Versus Life."

In case you are wondering why I am writing a book, the truth is that I am writing it for myself. Next, for other girls my age, and then for anyone who might want to read about the life and thoughts of a person like me. If some boy wants to read this, go ahead. Maybe you will learn something.

Barbara Fisher
87 Maple St.
Fair Park, N.Y., U.S.A.

1

I WILL BEGIN my book on the first day of school last fall, which was September 8, and rainy. It was an important day for our family. It was my first day at Jefferson Middle School. It was Richard's first day of eighth grade at Jefferson. It was the first day of elementary school at Washington School, where my father is principal. And it was my mother's first day at her first job in fifteen years! She was going to be a reporter on the *Plainview Journal*, which is a daily paper in Plainview County, where we live. It is not *The New York Times* or anything, but a lot of people read it.

"I don't know why I chose this day to begin," Ma said. "The first day of school always makes me nervous. I remember when each of you children went off to kindergarten for the first time. *You* were fine, but I could hardly eat."

"Want a piece of toast, Ma?" Richard asked.

"No thanks," Ma said. "I think I might throw up."

Dad said, "I always like the first day of school.

After we've been working all summer in that empty building without any kids, we get eager for them to come and make things real."

My father is unusually nice. He is forty years old. Once, on a dare, he ate eleven dishes of ice cream with chocolate sauce. My father likes to do things with Richard and me. He teaches us magic tricks. He helped us build tables for our rooms. He explains things, like how to understand what is fact and what is propaganda. He really cares about kids, and about learning things. I think he must be a very good principal.

Some negative things about my father are (not that I *want* to be negative, but I hate books where everybody's family is perfect. In this book I intend to tell the bad along with the good. That is called "realism."):

1. My father works awfully hard, and he always has meetings that go on too long, and he has to come home late for supper.

2. My father is *always* teaching. When he says, "You know, a really interesting thing is . . ." then you know he is going to explain something to you whether you want him to or not. Sometimes when he is helping me with math I just want to get it over with fast, but he'll say, "Look, an interesting thing is, if you change this number. . ."

3. My father gets really mad sometimes. If I'm fooling around when he wants to think, he some-

times shouts at me, "Damn it, shut up!" (I know fathers in books don't talk that way unless they are supposed to be deprived, or to show why the child is going to run away from home. Anyway, my father is nicer than fathers in books, and most other people's real fathers that I know.)

Ma said, "Did you both get your lunch money? And you have our phone numbers in case you need to get in touch. Barbara, are you really feeling OK about Jefferson?"

To be truthful, I was feeling a little scared, even though I had been to Jefferson lots of times for Richard's band concerts, and we had an orientation day there last spring and learned how to work the combination locks on our lockers and where to buy supplies. I was worried that I might get lost in the halls and be late for a class, or have my lunch hour when none of my friends did, or lose my identification card (or have to show it to somebody, with that horrible picture of me on it).

But I told Ma I would be fine. "You look nice," I said. "You will find many friends on your new job."

Ma laughed. That's what she and Dad always say when Richard and I go somewhere new: You are sure to find many nice friends.

Ma is a comforting kind of person. She always sits through bad dentist appointments with us, and goes to school to have conferences with our teachers, and brings us raspberry ice if we are sick. My mother is rather short—Richard is nearly as tall as she is. She is forty-one—yes, that is one year older than my father. (This makes a good example of how people think in stereotypes. Why shouldn't she be a year older than my father? But when I mention this fact, some people act as though my parents committed an offensive act when they got married.) Anyway, my mother and my father really like each other, which is more than I can say about some people's parents. When they fight, Richard and I do not have to worry that they are going to get divorced.

Some negative things about my mother are:

1. My mother yells at me some. She is very efficient and I am not. I try to remember to do what she asks me to, but sometimes I forget and then she gets impatient and yells.

2. She wants me to be happy, and sometimes I feel guilty if I'm not happy every minute, when she works so hard to make things right for me.

3. She won't let me have a dog. (Neither will my father.) It's not that she hates dogs, either. But she says she hates taking care of them all the time, and the way they bark when people come to the door, and having to take them on a vacation. "A dog is no vacation," Ma says. And she says, "Without a dog around, I am a nicer person and don't yell so much." That's true. But I want a dog very deeply, and I wish she could understand.

Dad said, "Well, Marian? Time for work." He went to get their coats out of the closet. "I really like this new schedule," he told Ma. "We'll have time to talk in the car every morning."

We had sort of a family hug in the middle of the kitchen. Ma said, "Have a good day, Richard. Have a good day, Barbara." She looked at us as though we were going to China.

Richard said, "Ma, we're fine. Have a good day yourself, and tell us about it at supper."

Richard is really nice. He is comforting, like Ma. I really love Richard, although (negative) sometimes I can't stand him. He is my only brother, and I don't have a sister, so he is very important to me.

Richard is good to share things with, especially things nobody but us would laugh at or understand, like the way kids in second grade always said, "You must be a fish, because your name is Fisher, ha, ha."

Or the way the girl who used to live next door made us whisper when we watched Lassie programs with her because she thought Lassie was too noble to interrupt.

Or the way our father has explained about a hundred times that redwood trees grow so old and tall because the bark of the redwood is fireproof. If I ask Richard why he won't lend me fifty cents, or why he drank up the last can of soda, he is likely to answer, "Because the *bark* of the *red*wood is *fire*proof." That just breaks us up.

Richard keeps his room absolutely perfect. He knows where he has put every issue of *Sports Illustrated* he has gotten since 1969, and he files all the letters he gets, including advertisements, in alphabetical order in a shoebox. He makes lists of things to do and he remembers to cross them off after he does them.

Lots of times Richard and I keep our radios at the same station and have our doors open and talk to each other across the hall. Richard and I are very different, but we share a lot of important things like our parents, and our house, and all the years of our past.

I am very lucky to have Richard for my brother.

Richard and I waved out the window as Ma and Dad drove down the driveway. Then we cleaned up the breakfast table a little and I brushed my hair one more time and we put on our raincoats. Mine is old and too short in the sleeves and I was sorry I had to wear it on the first day at Jefferson School. We fixed the latch on the front door so it would lock behind us, and went out.

Richard said, "Here we *go*, up the *road*, to a birthday par*ty*," which are the words to a song we learned in nursery school. We always say that when we're going someplace we worry about, like the dentist.

It was funny to walk down the driveway on the first day of school and not have anyone to look back at and wave to.

ON BOOKS VS. LIFE

I have noticed many differences between
books and real life. On the whole I don't
mind. I love to read about strange or
beautiful things that could never really
happen: enchanted swans, silver nutmegs,
glass slippers. I also like to read about
real things that would not happen to me,
like taking care of mountain goats in
meadows full of flowers.

What I do not like are "real life" stories
that are false. For example, stories about
Friendly Policeman Bob, or Jolly Farmer
Jones, that you know could never happen
because nobody is that kindly every minute.
Or little kids' books about cities where
all the houses are green or pink and have
white shutters. Or books that act as though
nobody ever goes to the A&P, or the toilet,
or gets stuck in traffic jams. Or those
books that never even mention the suburbs,
even though that is where an awful lot of
kids in America live.

There is another kind of book where all
the girls have fancy names. That may not
seem very important to you, but if your
name was Barbara Fisher, you might also get
tired of reading about people called Candy

or Connie or Amanda or Alison all the time.
Penny. Cindy. Patience. Hilary. I suppose somebody called Taffy could have a real
life, but it is hard for me to believe in a
girl who goes around being Taffy all
the time.

The worst kind of untrue "real life" book
is the kind where everything comes out neat
in the end, the way things do not in real
life. For example, a story where a girl
wants a horse, but her family is very poor,
so she enters a contest that has a horse
for a prize, and naturally she wins the
contest. But her family has no place to
put the horse, so some kind man gives her
father a job in the country, and the family
moves right out to a house that has a barn
behind it for the horse to live in. Hon-
estly! You would think somebody in that
family would say, "If you expect this whole
family to pack up and move fifty miles to
the country just because of some damn horse,
you are crazy." But nobody says that in
horse books.

Another thing happens to that girl who
won the horse. All through the book she is
not very pretty, but suddenly one day she
is out riding and she falls off the horse
and meets some boy who picks her up, and
her heart starts thumping. So she goes home
and brushes her hair a new way and the boy
calls her up for a date and she turns out
to be beautiful.

To tell you the truth, sometimes I think
it would be nice to turn out to be beautiful so easily in real life. But I have

enough sense to know that it only happens
that way in books.

The biggest difference between life and
books in my opinion is that in books people's wishes usually come true, although in
life they often do not. For example, my
deepest wish is for a dog. I wish what
always happens in books would really happen
to me, like this: "Suddenly, a little black
ball of curly fur, its red tongue hanging
out, its short tail thumping merrily,
hurtled into Barbara's arms . . ."

But my parents will not let me have a dog.
Which proves that real life is not like
books.

2

SCHOOL TURNED OUT to be good. By the end of the first day I knew how to get around. I kept meeting my friends in the halls between classes. I could work the combination lock on my locker. There was pizza in the cafeteria. Mary and I had three classes together. I knew I was going to like Miss Peretti.

The only bad thing was PE.

On the first day, you had to go to the gym when your schedule said PE and sign up for the class you wanted. There were lists of classes on the blackboard. The boys' list was about twice as long as the girls'.

Boys	Girls
soccer	field hockey
basketball	modern dance
tennis	acrobatics
track	slimnastics
touch football	
wrestling	

I love tennis, and I want to learn how to play right. I asked one of the women PE teachers if I could get into a tennis class.

She said, "But don't you see? That's listed under 'Boys'."

I asked, "Why?"

She said, "That's just the way it's listed. How about field hockey? That's a good outdoor sport."

I *hate* field hockey. I played it every day in fifth grade at Park Street School. Field hockey is the most boring game I ever played in my life. If you have to play fullback you just stand around and wait for something to happen. Anyway, field hockey didn't fit my schedule. Tennis would have. The only girls' class that fit was slimnastics.

I explained that to the teacher, and she said, "Well, that means you'll have to sign up for slimnastics, doesn't it."

I said, "I don't *want* to take slimnastics."

She said, "In school, we do many things we don't want to do. That is part of education. And to look at you I can see that slimnastics would be helpful. Your tummy sticks out."

If there is one word I cannot stand, it is *tummy*. I think it is the most vulgar word in the English language, except perhaps *nostril*. I would certainly never use it in conversation to insult someone.

I couldn't talk to that teacher any more, so I tried another one, a man.

"Can I take tennis?" I asked him.

He said, "No, tennis is boys only."

I asked, "How come?"

He said because the tennis *team* was for boys only.

I wanted to ask how come again, but he turned away to sign some boy's program card. I didn't know who else I could talk to, so I wrote slimnastics down on my schedule, and made out a schedule card, and got it signed. Later, I found out that two friends, Sandra and Sally, would be in the same class, so I didn't feel too bad.

At the end of the day I looked for Richard, but he wasn't on the bus. He had said he might stay after for basketball tryouts. I sat with Oliver and told him about no tennis for girls.

"That's crazy," Oliver said.

Oliver lives across the street from me. Sometimes we play tennis in a park near us. We learned how to score and hold a racquet in a summer rec program we went to when we were about eight, but we never really learned how to play. My serves always go into the net, and Oliver doesn't serve very well either, so it is hard to get any kind of a game going between us. If people come around while we are playing, we quit. We don't like anyone to see us.

Oliver was going to take touch football. That was a good idea, because there aren't enough people on our block to play touch football with. There are hundreds of little kids, but Oliver and Richard and I are the only grown ones.

The bus stopped around the corner, and Oliver and I walked home slowly. I love my street. It has big trees that spread over it and it's so quiet we can walk down the middle of the street and no cars come along. When we were little we played Kick the Can out there on summer nights. Sometimes we still do.

I was wishing I had a dog to run out and meet me when I came home. Then the house wouldn't seem so quiet. I unlocked the back door with the key we keep in the tool cupboard and went in. Of course I am much too old to be scared by an empty house, but I did feel sort of lonely. The kitchen table was just the way Richard and I had left it. The orange juice glasses had sticky orange stuff stuck on them. There were brown rings in the bottom of the coffee cups. Since there was no one but me around to clean up, I did it.

Then I went out to get the mail. It was a good day—two gift catalogues, the kind I love to read, with cuckoo clocks and magic plants that live on air, and Mr. and Mrs. Skunk salt and pepper shakers. One catalogue had a page of "Party Gags" with things like plastic vomit to fool people with. I got an apple and took off my shoes and sat down to read, but the phone rang. It was Richard. He asked me to do his paper route, because basketball tryouts were still going on and he wouldn't be home in time.

I had always wanted to do the paper route, but Richard would never let me—he had this perfect record of never missing a day, and he was determined not to spoil it. I used to plan how I would fill in nobly for him if he got sick, but Richard never gets sick. So this was my very first chance. I really liked the idea. Delivering papers makes you sort of a messenger of important news.

The pile of papers Richard had to deliver was already on our front walk. I had a hard time fitting them all into my bike basket, and when they were in I could hardly balance on the bike. I hadn't realized the papers would be so heavy. My front wheel wobbled when I started off and I was afraid I would fall and spill all the papers but I pushed hard and held on and by the time I was halfway down the block I had the hang of it.

All the Warner boys were sitting on their front lawn when I came past. They are five little boys from three to nine years old. They look about the same but I suppose Mrs. Warner can tell.

They all said, "Hey, Barbara!"

One of them said, "Hey, Barbara, you delivering the papers?" which he could easily see the answer to just by looking.

I went on. I wasn't going to spend time talking— I hadn't even talked to Oliver when I threw the paper at his house. It took Richard an hour to do the paper route, and I wanted to get home before dark.

Lorraine and Laverne Baskin, who I baby-sit sometimes, were climbing on their jungle gym. They yelled "Barbara, Barbara," the way they always do when I go past. They really like me. I stopped my bike and gave the paper to Lorraine. All the way down the street I could hear Laverne fighting with her about who got to carry the paper inside. Sometimes I think I would go crazy being a twin.

I had to keep stopping to check the names on Richard's list, so I was slower than he was. But it was really fun to deliver the papers. I got better at hitting doorsteps—only two papers fell off into bushes, and I got them out before anyone noticed.

At the end of the route, I put on my bike light to ride home. It was almost dark except for the orange-and-purple sunset in the sky behind me. I had delivered sixty-eight papers and I really felt good. There were yellow lights on in all the houses. But when I turned the corner into Maple Street, I could see that my own house was dark.

I went in and turned on a lot of lights. Then I looked in the refrigerator and found a package of pork chops. I began to brown them in the skillet. I opened a big pack of frozen peas, which I love, and put them in water on the stove, and then I made a salad and began to set the table. And then all of a sudden I heard Richard thumping up the front steps, and my parents' car driving up to the back door.

Ma came in and started taking off her coat and said, "That's about the nicest thing that's happened to me my whole first day, Barbara, coming home to see the lights on and find you fixing the supper." She gave me a kiss.

"How was school, Barbara?" Dad asked.

I said, "Fine. And I did the paper route for Richard, too."

Richard said, "Thanks for saving my honor. Neither rain nor hail nor snow nor basketball practice will keep the *Journal* from my customers."

Supper tasted delicious—maybe because I had made it myself. Ma told us about her work at the *Journal*. She would have her own desk and typewriter, and go out to interview people. But this day she had just written up two weddings and five funeral announcements. She said they'd be in the next day's paper, but they wouldn't have by-lines because weddings and funerals never do. (A by-line is your name at the top of the story: BY MARIAN FISHER.)

Dad said the first day at Washington School had been very calm, even though the building was all changed around, with chairs and shelves and books in the halls and open space in the rooms. They have open classrooms in his school now, which means that children don't have to sit at desks and not talk and all do the same work at the same time. They can move around when they need to, without asking a teacher. They go into other rooms, or into the hallways, for science projects, or art, or to do math problems with just one or two other kids, or to read with one teacher. Some of the teachers and my father had been working all summer to get things ready. Those kids don't know how lucky they are. At Park Street School we used to have to line up for everything, even when we were just going outside to play.

"How are your classes going to be?" Dad asked me.

I told about my day, including how I had to take slimnastics, because girls couldn't take tennis.

"That's absurd," Dad said.

"Do you want us to talk to the PE Department for you?" Ma asked.

I said no. I don't like my parents to come to school and ask for something, because my own father is a principal and I don't want anyone to think I get some kind of special privilege. That would be very embarrassing.

Richard said he had the best biology teacher in school, and his English class was going to read *Black Elk Speaks,* the true memories of an American Indian. Richard would have basketball tryouts for three more weeks, and if he made the team he would have practice every day.

"What about your paper route?" I asked him, thinking how perfect it would be if I could do it, because I love to ride my bike and delivering papers was fun and I needed the money. And even though I am sometimes sloppy, I knew I could be conscientious about the papers.

"Would you like to take over the route?" Richard asked.

"Oh, yes," I said.

"Well, if I make the team, it's yours," he promised.

When I went to bed that night, I was really happy. I had got through my first day at Jefferson and it was OK, and I had delivered the papers and fixed the whole supper, and now maybe I'd get the paper route for good! Richard made at least $5.75 a week and sometimes as much as $6.50 if people tipped him. I was thinking that I could buy records, and a special kind of jeans I wanted, and even save money for presents and things.

If I only had a dog, my life would have been just about perfect at that minute.

ESSAY

ON SIGNS

I often do not like signs.

I don't mind useful signs, like PUSH or
EXIT or HOSPITAL QUIET. But signs that are
supposed to be funny or cute, or tell you
to be happy, like SMILE, usually work back-
wards on me. When I see a sign that says
SMILE I suddenly feel grouchy. I always
wonder, who is telling me to smile—the
people who put the sign on the wall, or
the people in the factory who painted it,
or who? How did they know I would come
along at a certain time in the afternoon
and read their sign? How did they know I
wasn't smiling already?

There is one funny sign that I think is
pretty good. It's at Richard's barber,
where I don't usually like to go because it
is full of men and boys and even little
boys who look at you as though you have no
right to be there, even if you are just
coming to tell your brother where your
father parked the car. I also don't like
the barber's because it has those calendars
with undressed women, or women in underwear
that I feel sorry for because all the men
seem to be staring at them. Anyway, the
funny (to me) sign says: THE NAME OF OUR

CREDIT MANAGER IS HELEN WAITE.   IF YOU WANT
CREDIT, JUST GO TO HELEN WAITE.   Get it?
   The signs that really make me mad are the
ones that are untrue.   I can't understand
why people go to the effort of making signs
in big capital letters, if they are a lie.
For example, the sign in the A&P that says
BANANAS YELLOW, RIPE when all you have to
do is look at the bananas to see that they
are actually GREEN, HARD.   I have finally
figured out that what the store does is
leave the sign up all the time, and let the
bananas come and go beneath it, from hard
green to speckled mushy, to hard green
new ones.   So sometimes the sign and the
bananas match.   But most of the time, not.
   Another untrue sign is the one at the
cleaner's in the shopping center that says
OPEN.   You could go by at midnight and see
the sign hanging there on the door saying
OPEN.   It says OPEN on Sundays, and at 6:15
just after the store has closed for the
day.   I have seen people with my own eyes
get out of their cars with bundles of
clothes to be cleaned and try to open the
door and then have to put all their clothes
back in the car and take them home again. You
would think the store people would have
more sense.   If I had a young child who was
just learning to read I would certainly
stay away from that cleaner's.   I have tried
to get my mother not to go there as a pro-
test against the sign, but she says it's
the most convenient cleaner's and if the
sign bothers me it is my responsibility to
say something about it.   (But I am afraid

they would think I was crazy or something if
I said anything.)

Another kind of sign that makes me mad is
the one that says Go CHILDREN Slow. Do you
know those signs? For many years I have
wondered why those signs don't say Go Slow,
CHILDREN, in a straightforward way. I don't
know the answer, so I will end with that
mystery. You may now STOP reading this
essay. But you do not have to SMILE.

3

AFTER A COUPLE of days our family was used to the new schedule. It was sort of fun to do things differently. My mother worked late at the *Journal* on Wednesdays, so Dad said he would not schedule any meetings for those nights. The first Wednesday, he and Richard and I went to the A&P after supper and did a giant shopping. The store was almost empty so we zoomed up and down the aisles.

A woman named Mrs. Weston, who lives around the corner, saw us and made us stop by setting her basket right in our way.

"Is Mrs. Fisher sick?" she asked Dad.

Dad said No, she was fine.

"Oh, I thought she might be sick, since you're doing her shopping," Mrs. Weston said. I had the feeling she was checking our basket to see if we had bought good healthy food or not. Then she let us go by moving her basket closer to the soap powders. I watched her choose three different boxes. She must be very clean.

Richard and I did talk Dad into buying some things Ma never gets, like chocolate marshmallow cookies and canned spaghetti. Also, Dad bought two pounds of grapes at 99 cents a pound, and one mango that cost 99 cents.

Richard said we were having what the ads call a Shoppers' Jamboree.

Dad said it was not such a jamboree when it came to $54.72 at the check-out counter, and would either of us care to guess where the word "jamboree" comes from?

I guessed Africa. Richard guessed France. Dad said he was sure it was Australian.

While they were loading the bags into the shopping cart, I ran back down the aisle to the Special Dictionary Offer and found "jamboree" in Volume 4. I'll tell you the answer since this is not the kind of book where they interrupt the story with dumb questions like:

—Who do you think was right about the word source?
—Pretend you are Barbara. Write a paragraph about going shopping as she might write it.
—What was the purpose of the author in this section? Characterize the treatment: informative, humorous, imaginative.

"Jamboree" is a made-up word, from jam, plus half of "corroboree," a dance of Australian natives.

Dad said he had won, but Richard and I said No, since the word was only half Australian. So Dad refused to give Richard and me pennies for bubble gum because we were not fair (he said). Fortunately, I had two cents of my own and Richard and I chewed loudly all the way home. Dad said the smell reminded him of years ago when we were little.

Every day that week I delivered papers. I had the route memorized by now. The worst part was having to go past a horrible orange-colored chow dog with a runny nose and runny eyes who slurped after me in a disgusting way, yipping and snuffling, when I got near his house. Even though I am a dog lover, and want a dog of my own more than anything, I would not take a chow dog if someone offered me one free, and my parents said I could have it. Chows are the crossest dogs in the world, and the drooliest. The drool is always dripping from that mangy fur ruff around their necks. Ugh.

The way I handled the chow dog was, I rode past him very slowly so as not to get him excited, and threw the paper as quietly as I could, and then sped up suddenly and got away before he noticed anything. Even so, I could feel his little runny eyes on me all the way down the block, and hear him yipping till I turned the corner.

Most afternoons, Ma would be home when I got back from delivering papers. She would start supper and then sit down and read the *Journal* that she brought home with her. She says it is really interesting to read the paper when you work on it, because you know the news behind the news. Ma says the *Journal* is a good paper because it's lively. Mr. Pollachek, the news editor, likes to get people excited about county problems.

Richard was still going to basketball tryouts. He thought he might make the team but he hated to talk about it with us until he knew for sure. He wanted to make the team like anything. I kept hoping for him.

Dad was having lots of meetings. Some parents had started to complain about the open classrooms. Dad says parents worry when their children do different things in school than they did. All they know about school is what they remember about their own, and they feel sort of hurt if schools are different than they used to be. Dad says the way to help people understand the changes is to explain them over and over again, and then to wait and let parents see that their children will learn to read and do math just as well as children ever did. I can't understand why any parent would complain about open classrooms. If I ever have children, I would certainly not want them to have to sit in rows and raise their hands even to get a drink of water, the way we did at Park Street School.

At Jefferson, my classes were good. We had this

great art room, where sixth grade classes get to try out all kinds of materials—metal, paints, wood, papier mâché, string, chalk, charcoal, ceramics, everything. I was making a three-dimensional design out of colored string.

My social studies class was about the Far East. You can't imagine how interesting social studies is when you are grown up. In grade school, all we did in social studies was learn principal products. There is no more boring subject than principal products, unless it is state capitals. But in my Far East class we were learning about different religions, like Buddhism and Hinduism, and about the different ways people in different countries bring up their children, or treat their old people.

Then there was Miss Peretti's English class, which I will tell about soon. It was the best.

The worst was slimnastics.

4

SLIMNASTICS was horrible.

On days when I had PE I would wake up in the morning and think, "I have slimnastics today," and my whole day would be spoiled. The teacher really hated me. Her name was Mrs. Bream.

She was always saying, "Barbara! Please make an effort to be graceful and agreeable, like a little lady. We have no tomboys in slimnastics."

Yes, they did. They had me. If slimnastics is what ladies do, then I knew I was no lady. We spent the first two weeks of slimnastics doing exercises to a terrible song called "Chicken Fat." That may sound like a funny name to you, but there was nothing funny about trying to do these undignified exercises while a man sang:

> *Give* that Chicken Fat
> *Back* to the Chicken . . .
> Go, you Chicken Fat, go!*

The music kept getting faster and faster, and the man called out "Faster, faster!" He seemed to laugh

*From: "CHICKEN FAT (The Youth Fitness Song)" by Meredith Willson.
© 1961 *Frank Music Corp.* and *Rinimer Corporation.* Used by permission.

at you all through the song. There were real chickens clucking in the background. It was insulting.

I don't think anyone really liked slimnastics, but
some people hated it more than others. Sandra and
Sally are both pretty skinny, and they didn't seem
to mind too much. I am not exactly fat, but I am
what you might call "plump" or "chubby" if you
are the kind of person who uses those words.

Naturally, I would like to be slender and attractive. I always read those ads about losing weight
that have long stories, with Before and After pictures. First the person confesses how big she was,
*I was married to a cowboy, but I was as big as a
horse,* and then she tells how she discovered delicious candies that killed her appetite and she lost
100 pounds and went from Hips 40 to Hips 34. If I
lost 100 pounds I would be dead, but I wouldn't
mind losing three or four.

My mother says the only reducing aid I need is a
closed mouth. She says if I would be more careful
about snacks I would certainly lose weight, and that
anyway I will lose my fat stomach when I get older,
and have a nice figure. It's funny not to know how
you are going to look in the future. I keep watching
the eighth grade girls. They act so sure of themselves, as if they know they are real teen-agers, and
not this dumb age I am, which people call "pre-
teen" or "young junior" when they want to sell you
clothes. It's awful to have to go to one of those de-
partments and hunt for something that fits, and

have salesladies try to sell you "Little Princess" underwear and call you "dear."

The trouble with slimnastics was, it made you keep thinking about how you looked, instead of learning how to *do* something. When the Chicken Fat record stopped, we could hear tennis balls thunking against the wall of the boys' gym next door. I kept wishing I was next door.

Then Mrs. Bream would say something maddening: "Girls! You may not think exercise is important now, but some day soon you'll be wanting to look your very best for that special boyfriend. How are you even going to attract his attention if you don't *look* attractive? Remember, a girl's best asset is a slim figure and a straight posture. No one loves a fatty, girls."

Sandra and Sally would just giggle at her, but you can imagine how I felt.

Finally, I stayed after school and told Miss Peretti how much I hated slimnastics, and asked her what I should do. She said I should talk to my guidance counselor.

But when I went to see Mrs. Anderson I got into this long discussion which I never expected. It was like she was scolding me for something I didn't understand. She said, "Surely your mother is glad you are taking slimnastics, Barbara. To look at you, I can see it would be just the right class. Doesn't your mother want you to be slim and graceful?"

I said that both my mother and father were sorry I couldn't take tennis.

She said I must have misunderstood them.

I said I didn't misunderstand them.

Then Mrs. Anderson said, "Barbara, just think if everybody did all the same things, what a dreary old world this would be. Fortunately, boys like to do strong, manly things, and girls like to do graceful feminine things, and we are trying to guide you toward these appropriate things in school."

I couldn't understand her. I certainly didn't want to do the same things as everybody. I just wanted to take tennis. I said that men and women both play tennis, and they have mixed doubles in tournaments.

Mrs. Anderson said, "Barbara, at Jefferson School the official tennis team is made up only of boys, so it is logical to have classes to prepare boys for the team, isn't it?"

Then she said something that really made me furious. She said, "If you practice slimnastics regularly, maybe you will be pretty enough to be a cheerleader for the tennis team."

I wanted to explain carefully to Mrs. Anderson what was so unfair about what she had said. But I knew that if I tried to talk I would cry, and I was too mad to cry in front of Mrs. Anderson and have her try to comfort me. So I left.

5

I DIDN'T TELL my parents about that talk with the guidance counselor. I knew my father would be angry, and that he would go right up to school and make a fuss. I would be so embarrassed if he did that.

The next day in the cafeteria, I was talking about slimnastics with Sandra and Sally. We began to sing the Chicken Fat song for Mary and my friend Arlene from Miss Peretti's class, who were taking modern dance. They thought it was funny. They began to sing with us. Pretty soon people all over the cafeteria were singing along:

> *Give* that Chicken Fat
> *Back* to the Chicken . . .

It was funny, but it wasn't funny. Bobby Higham and Jim deRienzi came over and sang with us. They both have older sisters. I guess that song has been famous for a long time. It is amazing to me that nobody ever complained about it before.

Bobby was taking tennis. He asked me why I didn't take tennis if I hated slimnastics so much.

I explained the whole thing.

"That isn't fair," Bobby said.

Jim said, "Well, there's probably some good reason. Like, girls can't take football or baseball or track, either."

I said, "Yeah, and why not? I love baseball."

Sally said, "Me, too."

And Arlene said, "I was the best pitcher in my old neighborhood. Everybody knew it."

Jim said, "But now you're in sixth grade and you're supposed to stop being tomboys. That's why they have all those modern dance classes and all, so you can learn to be graceful. If you like sports, you can go out for cheerleader."

"For goodness' sake!" I yelled. "I don't *want* to be a cheerleader! Why does everybody think all every girl wants is to be a cheerleader? I think cheerleaders are *stupid*. All I want is a chance to learn tennis in school, what's wrong with that?"

Jim looked at me with this really maddening smile and he said, "Hey, Barbara, you're not turning into one of those women's lib nuts, are you?"

Boy, did that make me mad. It was bad enough for things to be so unfair, without being called a nut for saying so. A women's lib nut.

Sandra said, "She isn't a nut. PE at Jefferson really is unfair to girls."

35

Jim said, "Well, anyway, she sure can use a class in slimnastics."

I said, "Oh, shut up, Jim."

Jim said, "Come on, let's not fight with a bunch of girls." He and Bobby went off.

We all said, "Good-by, good riddance," and things like that. Lunch period was over. Sally said, clearing off her tray, "Listen, Barbara, let's start a campaign to have girls' tennis at Jefferson. We could make a petition—"

I said, "Well, I have no desire to stand up and make speeches and have people like that dumb Jim deRienzi call me a loud-mouthed nut, that's for sure."

But I was thinking that it *would* be good if we could make some changes, by working for them ourselves. So while we were walking down the hall, Sally and I began to figure out what a petition should say.

I guess that lunch time was my real introduction to thinking about women's liberation, or girls' liberation. Of course I had read about equal rights in the newspaper, but I had never really connected that to anything I would do. I used to think there was something sort of embarrassing about women's liberation. People were always making jokes about women burning their bras, and expecting you to laugh. The only bra I had was called "Little Miss Beginner," which is about the only kind that fits somebody my age, and I was certainly not going to burn it. I just never thought that women's liberation had anything to do with me.

But suddenly I started to notice how many times people said "girls don't do that" about something I wanted to do, or acted as though girls like me were stupid or foolish when we tried to stand up for our rights. It seemed like a funny coincidence that these things all began to happen at once.

I know it is hard to believe in coincidences in books, even though you will believe almost any amazing fact in the paper, like a woman loses her diamond ring and forty years later she eats a sausage and breaks her tooth on something hard and it is her diamond ring.

I'm not talking about that kind of coincidence. It's just that suddenly I began to notice how many things were unfair to girls, and how angry people got if you complained about it. Maybe it wasn't coincidence so much as just that I had never noticed before. But now, I was really noticing.

6

RICHARD MADE THE basketball team!

He ran into the kitchen to tell us, dribbling a pretend ball around the table, and twisting to shoot it up at some imaginary basket on the ceiling.

"Yea, Fisher!" I yelled.

I thought it would be fun to go to games and say, "That's my brother," when the team came out on the court for warm-up. Or, just casually after Richard made some spectacular shot, "That was my brother." "Your *brother*? Wow!"

We were all proud of Richard. Ma and Dad wrote down the date of his first game in their date books, so they would be sure not to work late or have meetings that night. Richard said he would give me a little wave when the team came out on the court before the game. But first, he was going to have weeks of practice, starting right after school and going on till supper time. So, of course, he wouldn't be able to do his paper route any more.

"What about the paper route?" I asked.

"Let's call the *Journal* and tell them you're going to do it from now on," Richard said.

He got out his record book, where he kept lists of all his customers' names and the payments for every week. So far, he had made $124.27! Then he dialed the *Journal*'s number and asked for the circulation manager. He said he wanted to give notice of giving up his paper route, and that he had someone to recommend. "She's already done the route lots of times and she knows the routine, so you wouldn't have to train her. Her name is Barbara Fisher, she's my sister."

Then he handed me the phone. But when I got it up to my ear the circulation manager was saying, "But Richard, we don't use girls as paper carriers. It's against the rules."

Coincidence! I could hardly believe it.

I said, "You are speaking to *Barbara* Fisher, not Richard Fisher. Can you tell me why it is against the rules for girls to deliver papers?"

Richard looked surprised.

The man said, "That's just the rule, honey. I don't make the rules myself, of course. But that's the way we've always done it, and I'm sure we can't make any exceptions. Besides, the newspapers would be much too heavy for a girl to manage on a bicycle."

I told him I had carried those papers on my bike every day for two weeks, and they weren't too heavy for *me*.

He said, "Well, don't tell anybody you did that, honey, because girls aren't *supposed* to do that and we don't want to get into trouble. Now, let me talk to your brother again."

Imagine calling somebody "honey" while you are insulting them! I gave the phone back to Richard. The circulation manager kept talking. Then Richard said, "The only other boy in this neighborhood over ten years old is Oliver Smith. I know he wouldn't do it. He takes care of about seven yards." Then there was a pause. I could hear the circulation manager's voice going on and on. Richard was shaking his fist and making faces at the receiver.

Then he said, "All right, I'll take care of it for a few weeks longer. No, I don't have another recommendation. I have already recommended a good person, and you are missing a real opportunity if you don't hire her." Then he slammed down the phone like an angry executive on a TV show.

"How can they be so dumb!" he said.

I was disappointed about the money, and the fun of doing the route. But I was really angry, besides. For two weeks I had been doing the paper route as well as any boy. What right did that man have to say I couldn't do it at all?

Richard said, "What are you going to do, Barbara?"

I hadn't thought of doing anything, except be mad.

"One thing you ought to do," Richard said, "is keep on delivering papers while the *Journal* finds somebody else. Then you can at least get *some* money."

"What if somebody tells on me?" I said.

Richard pointed out that nobody had complained yet.

I said that was true. "In fact," I remembered, "when I collected money last week, a couple of people even said it was nice I was doing the route. Like Mrs. Baskin." Then I had an idea.

"Maybe I could get testimonials from the customers!"

Richard said, "Hey, yeah, maybe you could take some kind of petition around when you collect on Friday."

A petition! Another coincidence. Do you know that the word "petition" comes from begging? Here I was, already begging for changes in PE at Jefferson, and now I was going to be begging to take over the paper route. And I shouldn't have had to beg for those things at all. They should be my rights.

Ma and Dad were upset when we told them what the circulation manager had said.

"Maybe I can talk to him," Ma said.

"Oh, no, Ma, don't do that," I told her. "I don't want to use your influence."

But Ma said that the circulation part of the paper had nothing to do with her job, and she would try to make time to talk to the circulation manager.

I said that I was going to ask for recommendations from the paper route customers.

Dad said, "I'd give you one myself, but someone might think I was prejudiced. As a matter of fact, I am. I think you're a very nice girl and a very good worker."

I said, *"Thank* you!" It really makes me feel good when my dad says things like that. He is a very praising kind of father. To tell you the truth, I think my family helped me very much in the coming days, just by treating me like a normal, ordinary human being. Because sometimes it seemed as though everybody else in the world thought I was a nut.

7

FIRST OF ALL, there was the PE petition. Sandra and Sally and I wrote the first part, about slimnastics:

```
    We believe that no girl should have to
take slimnastics unless she wants to.
But at some periods there are no girls'
PE classes except slimnastics. We be-
lieve that classes like tennis and vol-
leyball should be given at these periods
too, so there is more choice.
```

Mary and Arlene thought we ought to ask for changes in the whole PE program while we were at it.

"What about all the boys' teams this school has?" Mary reminded us. "Football, basketball, track, wrestling . . ."

I said, "I hate football. It doesn't bother me not to be able to take football. Any boy who's dumb enough to play football can have it."

Arlene said that wasn't the point. "Don't you see, it's the *idea*—it's like football is the most important

43

thing in our whole school, and it's just for boys. The whole football business—pep rallies, marching band, cheerleaders, everybody in town going crazy on game days—is just so a bunch of boys can go out on a field and beat each other up. I bet half the PE money at Jefferson goes for football coaches and uniforms and equipment."

"And only a few boys make the team, but football's supposed to teach all of us sportsmanship," Sally added. "It's crazy. You could take the money they spend on football and build a swimming pool for everybody to use."

"Or you could have a lot more school teams, for girls *and* boys," I said. I had never thought about this before. "You could have a girls' tennis team and a mixed doubles team, besides a boys' team. Then they'd have to have tennis classes for girls."

We got excited about these ideas, and we added some new parts to the petition.

> We believe that the entire sports program at Jefferson is based on boys' teams, and that this is not fair to girls. We believe that girls should compete in sports themselves, and not just be cheerleaders for the boys.
>
>   We ask the PE department to look into this matter and to talk with student representatives about changing their program.
>
>   SIGNED

"Do you think we ought to talk to some gym teachers first?" Sally asked. But we decided we should get signatures first, to show the gym teachers that lots of people agreed with us. We made a very neat copy of the petition, and taped an extra sheet of paper to it, to hold all the signatures we thought we would get. Arlene and I were going to take turns holding the petition. I said I would go first.

We were so dumb, we never imagined that people wouldn't agree with us. We certainly didn't expect them to *laugh* at us.

The very first girl I showed the petition to, laughed.

"What's the matter," she said. "Didn't you get picked for cheerleader?"

She grabbed the petition and took it over to a bunch of her friends who were sitting on the grass. They started giggling.

"Are you kidding?" one of them said, looking over at me and Arlene.

"This is crazy!" another girl said. "Hey, Cathy, this is a petition for no cheerleaders!"

A girl in a green Jefferson cheerleader jacket looked up, shrugged, and turned away. She didn't even look at the petition.

One girl said her boyfriend would kill her if she signed anything against football.

"What's the matter with slimnastics?" some boy

asked. "You want girls to take football instead?"

I grabbed the petition back. So far, it only had two names on it: Arlene's and mine. A teacher, I think named Miss Marcy, came out.

"Would you like to sign this petition?" I asked her. She was carrying a big pile of books, so I held the petition up where she could read it. When she had finished, she shook her head.

"No, thanks," she said, very polite.

"Don't you agree?" Arlene asked her.

"No, I don't," she said. "The Physical Education Department has its own reasons for its programs and I wouldn't want to interfere. PE is not my province."

Some girls from my slimnastics class came out. I took the petition over and they read it, but one of them said, "I like slimnastics OK," and they all just walked on.

It was a relief when Sandra came out looking for us. We ran over to her and yelled, "Wanna sign a petition?"

"How many did you get?" she asked, and then she looked at the empty petition. "Nobody else?"

"Nobody."

Sandra signed. I was glad to see even one more name on that blank piece of paper.

Suddenly lots of kids came out of school. I was beginning to wish I wasn't standing there with that petition. If my friends hadn't been there, I think I might have just gone away. It makes you feel so funny and conspicuous to keep going up to people and asking them to read what you wrote and agree with it. And it makes you feel worse when they don't agree.

I saw one girl waiting by herself, so I went over. "Sign?"

She read the petition carefully. "Got a pencil?"

I couldn't believe it. I gave her my pencil.

She signed. "Irene Norton."

"Hope you get a lot," she said. "I always wanted to take tennis, and they never would let me."

"Hey, me too!" I said. "That's why we started this whole thing, because there isn't any tennis for girls, and you have to take slimnastics."

She laughed. "Disgust! I took slimnastics for two years. 'Go, you Chicken Fat, go.' "

Some boys came up and stood behind her.

"What's that, Irene?" one of them said. He grabbed the petition and began to read it.

"What is this?" he said. "Only some kind of nut would make a petition against football. This school *always* has football. Football makes our school have school spirit."

The other one said, "What's the matter with cheerleaders? I *like* cheerleaders." He gave this self-satisfied laugh.

I just hated those boys. How could you explain anything to them? Irene started to walk away with them, but she gave me a look over her shoulder, and sort of a wink.

Some girl pulled the petition out of my hand. "You'll get into trouble with this," she said, handing it back. "They aren't going to change the whole PE program just to please some nut."

"I'm not a nut!" I shouted.

"You are, if you think you can change things," she said.

Arlene and Sandra had been standing across the walk, watching. They came over and Arlene asked if I was ready to give up.

I was, but I said No. I said I'd keep the petition in my locker while we decided what to do next.

Mary and I walked to the bus together. Mary said, "At least we aren't back at Park Street School, being daffodils in some play."

"Or learning 'Sail on, sail on and on' for Columbus Day," I said, squinting my eyes to look for America the way we used to have to. "But I sure am glad it's Friday. I am ready for a good long rest."

I had forgotten that Friday was collection day on my paper route.

8

AS USUAL, THE house was empty when I got home— Dad and Ma at work, Richard at basketball practice. I made myself a pitcher of frozen orange juice and a peanut butter sandwich.

Then I sat down at the kitchen table with Richard's newspaper list. I wondered how I could face all those people I didn't know—Mr. Rodney Johnson, Mrs. Ruth Kamm, Mr. Earl Lipkin—and ask them to recommend me for the paper route job. After my experience with the PE petition I didn't feel like asking anyone to do anything. I thought how nice it would be to glide by all the houses on my bicycle, completely invisible, throwing papers from a great distance and riding on through the twilight like a secret messenger.

Instead, I was going to go up to strange people's doors and make myself conspicuous: "I'm Richard Fisher's little *sister*, blah blah, and the *Journal* doesn't want girls to deliver the *paper*, but I'm so good, blah, blah, please recommend me." Ugh.

I had to do it. In one or two more weeks, the paper route would go to some boy and I'd never get the chance to prove that I could deliver papers as well as Richard. And I wouldn't earn all that money.

I washed my face and brushed my hair hard, to make a good impression. In the mirror, I looked like an ordinary girl, even the kind somebody might call "a nice little girl." For good luck, I brushed my teeth too. Then I went downstairs and put on my jacket and got out my bike and loaded the papers into the basket, and started off.

I had decided the best way was to get recommendations from people on my block who knew me, and after that to ask anybody else who smiled or looked sympathetic when I collected the money.

I went to Oliver's house first. I knew Mrs. Smith would write something nice about me if I asked her. She's known me all my life. If I ever got a nosebleed at school and my mother wasn't home, Mrs. Smith would come to school and take me back to her house and give me a blanket on the couch, and be kind. She must have made me about as many Saturday lunches and after-school sandwiches as she made for Oliver. When we were little, Oliver and I used to get double snacks by going to his house and saying, Can we make popcorn, and then eating it and going over to my house and asking, Can we make popcorn. But that ended one Saturday morning when we had buckwheat pancakes and syrup at my house and then we went to Oliver's and had regular pancakes with peach jam and bacon, and I threw up. Mrs. Smith called my mother and they figured that we must have eaten about fourteen pancakes each. After that, we had to promise just to eat one meal each at any one mealtime.

Oliver came to the door. I explained what I was doing. He said his mother wasn't home.

"Listen, Barbara," he said, "I'll write you a note and sign it in an official-looking way. Nobody'll know that a kid wrote it."

He went off and got some real stationery from his mother's desk, and a pen. We sat down on his front steps while he worked on the note.

Oliver has been my friend for a very long time. He doesn't care whether I am a girl or not. Kids used to tease us all the time when we were in second grade and third grade and those, which is a time when some people think it is almost against the law for a boy to walk down the street with a girl. Kids used to yell at us: Oliver likes Barbara! Ha, ha, Oliver! and things like that. I just hated it. One reason I liked Oliver so much is that I know he hated it too, but he never stopped walking home with me after school.

Oliver wrote a good note. It said:

Barbara Fisher is a very trustworthy, cooperative, nice, paper deliverer. I and my family very sincerely reccommend her to you, and hope she will deliver our paper for many years to come.

Sincerely yours,

Oliver Smith

(Later on, I discovered he had spelled recommend wrong but I didn't change it since many grownups are bad spellers.)

I was two houses down the block when I remembered that I hadn't given Oliver their *Journal,* or collected money from him. I decided to go on, and do it on the way home.

I went to the Baskins' next. Lorraine and Laverne were at the top of their jungle gym and they both began turning somersaults in a hurry to get down. Lorraine jumped off first and ran up to me and bumped into my stomach while I was fixing the kickstand on my bike. About ten papers bounced out of the basket.

"You knocked the papers out!" Laverne yelled, running up. She didn't pick any up, though.

"I did not!" Lorraine said. I have noticed that little kids say "I did not" automatically, even when it is clear that they *did.* Anyway, Lorraine began to help me pick up the papers.

I said, "I have to talk to your mother."

I held the Baskins' paper and my collection list in one hand. The twins held onto my other hand and pulled me along to the house.

"Hello, Barbara," said Mrs. Baskin. "You've come for the money. Just a second." She went to get the money, and Lorraine and Laverne began to tell me the news.

"Guess what, Barbara, Mommy's going out Sunday night and you're going to baby-sit."

"Guess what, Barbara, I had a tuna fish sandwich."

"Hey, Barbara, I can hang onto the top of the jungle gym with one hand, wanna see me?"

"Guess what, my Daddy's coming home in ten minutes!"

"No, half an hour!"

"Ten minutes!"

"Half an hour!"

I have always thought that the saying "two's company" ought to be changed for the Baskins. With them, two's a crowd.

All of a sudden, they stopped yelling and ran off to the jungle gym. They can't stand to be anywhere longer than five minutes.

Mrs. Baskin came out with the money. I checked her name on my list and explained how I was trying to get the paper route.

She said she'd be glad to write me a recommendation.

There was a shriek from the girls. Mr. Baskin's car had turned into the driveway.

"Daddy, Daddy!"

"Daddy!"

"Oh, excuse me, Barbara, I'll have to go," Mrs. Baskin said. "Mr. Baskin just doesn't like his supper to be late. I'll give you your recommendation the next time you come by."

If I were Mrs. Baskin, I would tell Mr. Baskin to cool it and learn to wait five minutes for his supper. Not that it's any of my business. But I know that if I get married, it will not be to some man who bosses me around the way Mr. Baskin bosses Mrs. Baskin, that's for sure. I will find a man who knows how to cook his own supper.

Two of the papers that had fallen out of my bike basket were all muddy, so I threw them away in the Baskins' garbage can. I always had a few extras to spare.

For once, all the Warner boys were inside. But when I rang the bell they rushed out on the porch.

"Hey, Barbara, you collecting paper money?"

"You want your money, Barbara?"

"Mommy! Barbara wants the paper money!"

Mrs. Warner came out, drying her hands on a kitchen towel. She had to push the door into boys to open it.

"Boys!" she said. "Let Barbara come inside, for goodness' sake."

She took my money out of a dish on the hall table. "Are you going to keep on doing the paper route?" she asked me.

I explained about Richard's basketball practice, and how much I wanted the route and the paper didn't want to give it to me.

"That's terrible!" Mrs. Warner said. "You want me to call them up?"

I said that would be very helpful, and Mrs. Warner said she would call the first thing Monday. She wrote it down on her calendar.

I ducked out around the boys and went back to my bike. They called after me: "You going to collect the rest of the money, Barbara?" and "Good-by, Barbara!" and so on. I waved, and pedaled off.

I was feeling much better. Talking to people I know had been easy. They all treated me like a perfectly reasonable person. I began to think it might not really be so hard to convince the *Journal* that I could have the route. Why wouldn't they change their rule, if the customers demanded it?

But on Spring Street, things were different. Spring Street isn't really my neighborhood. There are a lot of new houses and people that I don't know. When I was little, this part of Spring Street was all briar-rose tangles, with gigantic thorns that tore your clothes or your skin if you tried to take a short cut through them. There was a pond farther along that you could get to from the street. Oliver and I used to ice skate there in the winter. It was just big enough for three or four people to skate on without bumping into each other. We were allowed to skate without any grownups because the water underneath was only about two inches deep. It was fun.

Now Spring Street has two rows of white houses with blue and sometimes bright pink shutters and funny little windows like portholes over the front door, as though they were ships at sea. To make a place for the houses they had to cut down all the big trees, and then the people who bought the houses had to set in little new trees and start all over again. The chow dog lives three houses down Spring Street.

I began at Crowell, the first house. I had never seen anyone at home there. I rang the bell but nobody came, so I put the paper in the screen door, with the bill folded up inside it.

At the next house, Johnson, a woman came to the door and smiled at me. But when I told her I wanted to do the paper route regularly, and asked her for a recommendation, she said, "Well, dearie, I don't sign anything these days. I'm sure you'll get the route if you behave well."

Behave well! What did she expect me to do, get drunk and throw the papers in the trash?

The chow began to bark before I even got near its yard. I started calling "That's a nice doggie, good doggie," and other complete lies. When I am scared of a dog I try to use this calm voice you are supposed to use so a dog knows you aren't scared. But I always know the dog knows that I know that he knows I really *am* scared. Anyway, I kept on saying "good doggie," and the chow calmed down a little bit, just snuffling around my shoes when I went down his front walk. But when I rang the doorbell he got very excited and started jumping up on me, rubbing that awful drool all over my jacket. I knew if I pushed him away someone would be sure to see me, so I made little patting motions at him. I thought I ought to act like a real chow dog fan if I wanted the owners to give me a recommendation.

A man stuck his head out the door and said, "What you want?"

I told him I was collecting money for the paper.

"Where's the boy?" he demanded.

I explained that Richard had given me the route, but the *Journal* said I couldn't have it. I asked him if he would recommend me. All this time the chow was snuffling and yipping, and jumping up on me.

The man said, "I don't know. A boy, you can depend on when the weather gets bad. A girl, I don't know."

Can you imagine? I was so insulted I could hardly stand there waiting for my paper money. When the man gave it to me I took it and walked straight back to my bike, with that darn dog tripping and snuffling over me all the way. When I got on my bike, ready to ride away fast, I finally shouted out what I had been holding back for two weeks:

"You stupid dog! You are the dumbest, drooliest, most revolting animal I ever met!"

Going on down Spring Street I got more and more discouraged. Either people weren't home, or they didn't have money and said they'd pay me next week. Nobody smiled, and I didn't ask for any recommendations. I wondered whether I was crazy to want the paper route in the first place.

After Spring Street, the paper route turns off into these streets with girls' names: Beryl Street, Alma Street, Annette Street, that some builder must have named after his kids. Too bad he didn't have better taste in names. I can see giving real people's names to boats or to dogs, but I think it is ridiculous to name streets after un-famous people. I know one street in Fair Park that a man who developed it named after *himself,* and guess what his name is? Sniffen. Can you imagine having to say, "I live at 97 Sniffen Street?" I would die. Maple Street may not be the most original name in the world, but at least it is pretty—and true.

Beryl, Alma, and Annette were bad-luck streets for me. Nobody wanted to write me a recommendation. They just gave me the money and shook their heads. At one house, a woman asked if my mother knew I was out. As though I had sneaked away from home to deliver newspapers!

It was almost dark. I had five more houses to go and a long ride home. I was all alone on the street, looking in the windows of people's houses and feeling the wind blow colder. My nose felt sniffly and my eyes were watering.

I just asked for a recommendation at one more house, where the woman who came to the door was wearing jeans. She looked pleasant, so I took a chance and explained. But she said, "Oh, I don't think so, dear. When the weather gets colder you'll want to stay inside and gossip with your friends. A girl just isn't tough enough to do a paper route day after day. I'm sure that's why the *Journal* makes its rule. We don't want to miss a single paper, you know."

That was so intolerant! Even if she called me "dear." I notice that people often use words like that when they are saying something mean. How did that woman think she could guess how tough I was?

Even though my bike basket was empty, the ride home seemed awfully long and cold. I was so angry that I could hardly keep pumping. I kept thinking about the unfairness of what people had said to me. I just *hate* it when people are unfair. Why should people think boys are reliable and girls aren't? I knew that I could be conscientious and reliable every single day if I had the paper route. But how could I prove it?

My hands felt cold on the hand brakes when I finally got back to my street. I could see a light in the kitchen at my house—my mother had just come home. I couldn't wait to go in and get warm and tell her what had happened. But when I turned into the driveway, Ma came out the front door to meet me.

"Barbara, Marilyn Smith just called and said there must be some mistake about their paper. They never got one. You'll have to take one over to her right away."

I didn't even have to look in my basket to know that there wasn't an extra paper left. The extras were in the Baskins' garbage can covered with mud. That's how reliable and conscientious I had been— I had thrown away the Smiths' newspaper a whole hour ago!

I stood in the driveway and cried.

Ma came down the steps and hugged me, and I told her what had happened. She said, "Barbara, it's all right, you just take them my paper. They'll never know."

So I wiped my face and she got me her *Journal*— it was nice and crisp because she hadn't even un-folded it yet—and I ran over to the Smiths' and gave the paper to Oliver and ran back home and took off my jacket and sat down at the table and drank a big glass of milk that my mother poured for me.

I think that must have been the longest day of my whole life.

ESSAY

ON TALKING TO YOUNGER PEOPLE

This is an essay for those who, because of their business or profession or their way of life, have occasion to come in contact with people between the ages of ten and nineteen. (I am writing as a kind of expert, since I myself am between those ages.)

Many warnings could be given about talking to someone this age, such as: Never use the word "youth." But in this essay I will just give one important piece of advice. This is it: Do not ever ask "What are you going to be when you grow up?"

This is an offensive question, partly because somebody who has grown all the way from an infant to, say, age eleven, thinks they are pretty grown up already. But it is also offensive because it is so personal. Can you imagine what would happen if some kid just went up to an adult, like a relative, or a neighbor or even a stranger in a store and asked them, "Please tell me, what are your secret hopes and wishes?" The adult would be offended, that's what.

I have not figured out why people think they have the right to ask you this kind of question just because you are younger than

they are. If you have never thought about
this, and you are an adult, I hope you will
think right now, and make a resolution not
to ask any kid a question you would not
want to answer yourself. This should aid
your communication with younger people.

I will close by stating that if you have
ever asked me what I wanted to be when I
grow up, and I told you "an animal doctor",
it was a lie. I use that answer because it
sounds like something a kid would want to
be and it satisfies people, so they stop
bothering you and say "Isn't that nice!"
and they feel that now they have approved
and so it is OK for you to go ahead and be
an animal doctor.

I am probably going to be a psychologist
or a writer or a teacher. I don't know
which right now, and I don't plan to decide
until it is time to decide. I am only telling you this because you didn't ask me.

9

I WOKE UP at school time, as usual, on Saturday morning. I don't mind doing that—otherwise I wouldn't know it was Saturday. It's such a luxurious feeling to roll over and go back to sleep, and know you don't have to run for the school bus.

When I did get up, my father was cooking breakfast. He makes these surprise omelets—you never know what you will bite into on the first chew, maybe a piece of salami or tomato, or a chunk of garlic. My father says his entire cooking secret is, "Double the garlic."

Ma and Richard were already eating.

"Sit down, Barbara," Dad said. "Here comes your high-protein cheese omelet, to give you strength for the work ahead."

I had forgotten it was Basement Clean-up Day, but I didn't mind. I was glad to have a day off from my own problems. Our basement may be a mess, but it's a comfortable kind of a mess.

Once Oliver's mother and Ma had a contest about

whose basement was worse. Oliver and I were supposed to be the judges, but we couldn't decide. We each voted for our own. At that time Oliver's father was raising mushrooms and baby chickens in his basement, so you can see how bad ours had to be to match that.

Our basement is full of boxes and paint cans and painting clothes, tied-up papers for the paper drive, a trunk of baby clothes, and two suitcases of presents from my parents' wedding. (Ma says they should have gotten rid of them right after they were married. Now she feels guilty about giving them away because they are sentimental, even though she hates silver trays and elephant bookends. Richard and I say that when it is our parents' silver wedding anniversary we will give them lovely presents right out of the basement.)

Then there are boxes and boxes of old photographs that never got sorted, some files of my father's school notes, and a box of Richard's and my school papers that Ma wants to save. There are shelves full of *National Geographic* magazines and some books that we've grown out of but want to have around in case we feel like reading them again. We have some really good books down there. Some of them are books Ma and Dad had when they were little, like *Wild Animals I have Known,* or *Tanglewood Tales,* and some of them are books that they read over and over to Richard and me, like *The*

Tale of Peter Rabbit or *Goodnight, Moon,* and all the *Little House* books. Richard and I have made Ma promise never to give these books to a library. That may sound selfish, but I can't help it. People always talk about books that stretch your mind. I need books that comfort my mind, too. I am beginning to read a lot of real books without age levels on the jacket. Some of them are hard to understand and some are scary. It is really nice to take a break in the middle of some confusing book and go down to the basement and find *The Peterkin Papers* and read about the Peterkins' Fourth of July one more time.

Dad said, "First, let's get the newspapers out of the way, and then we can sort the paint and throw out some of the painting clothes. They're beginning to smell moldy."

Ma said, "I wish we could get some of our old pictures organized. It makes me feel terrible not to be able to find the one I want. I think our last scrapbook ended with Barbara's fourth birthday."

"That's seven years ago," I said. "You mean we have seven years' worth of pictures downstairs?"

"Worse," Ma said. "We have pictures of my family, your Aunt Mary and Uncle Charles, and even some of my aunts and uncles and cousins, and lots of pictures of me at college and pictures of Daddy and me before we were married—"

"Can I do them?" I asked. "Let me bring them

upstairs and spread them out in the dining room and sort them, OK?"

"Well," Ma said. "If you'd dust the boxes before you carry them up, and promise to finish the job once you start."

Richard said, "I don't see why I should carry stuff up and down stairs all day if all Barbara has to do is sit and sort pictures."

Dad said that I should help with the papers and the paint and paint clothes before I did the photos. "Then you and I," he said to Richard, "can look into some of the boxes of junk. I'm sure there are good things in those boxes and I'm ready to say Finders keepers to whoever goes through them. You might find some usable tools, or some boxes for your desk."

(Richard and my Dad are like Eeyore: they both love containers and boxes and Useful Things to Put Things In.)

Richard said, "I could go through the old toy boxes, too. Maybe I could find some things to give away. I'll bet we have three complete sets of *Candyland*, at least."

Candyland! We used to love that game. It's really stupid. All you do is move a marker along a board. But the board has pictures of candy canes and ice cream cones and gumdrops and we used to think it was wonderful. It's funny how innocent little kids are. Candy is just about all they need to make them happy, or even the *idea* of candy. I'm glad I'm not a little kid anymore.

Sorting all our pictures made me think about children and grownups and past times and the future. It's so strange to look at a picture of a little baby and realize that it's your*self*, the same self you are now, and the self you will be when you arc old. Miss Peretti read us a poem that said,

the child is father of the man

and I think that's an interesting and mysterious idea. Just think: that little baby, Barbara Fisher, three weeks old, was kind of a mother to the girl I am now and the woman I am going to be someday. All of them are me.

I was lucky—I am lucky—to have my parents for parents. I found a picture of Dad sitting on our porch showing Richard and me an inch worm on his hand. He looks so *interested* in the worm, and so loving to us. I can't even remember that time, but I recognize my father, being just like himself.

In another picture Ma is standing under a tree watching Richard climb up it. Richard is very little. You can tell Ma is scared but she is smiling up at him. She used to have a rule about tree-climbing: "Don't go up if you can't get back down." She made the rule because Richard and I always climbed higher than we really meant to, and then yelled for Ma or Dad to get us down.

"We won't always be around to get you out of trees," Ma told us.

That's true. I'm glad she wasn't the kind of mother who says Don't climb, though.

I put the pictures from Ma's family on one side of the table, and from my dad's on the other side, and I made piles of our own family's pictures by years. Some of our years I remember and some I don't but I love all the pictures. I found some nice ones of Richard holding me when I was just born. I am very tiny and my legs stick out of my rubber pants holes like little toothpicks. My hair is all furry. Richard is holding me with this amazed and confused and proud look on his face. I found the negative to one of those pictures, and I'm going to pay to get a print made for my bulletin board. I also found a baby picture of Richard with no clothes on that he will just hate, and I am going to get myself a print so I can blackmail him from time to time.

I found a beautiful picture of my father's grandmother, my great-grandmother, Adelaide Crawford, taken when she graduated from high school in Toledo, Ohio in 1892. Her hair is piled on top of her head. She is wearing a black dress with big sleeves, and a proud smile. She was the first girl in the family to graduate from high school—her older sisters had quit to work in the knitting mill when they were fifteen. But Adelaide went on to college, and became a teacher, and married a man from Al-

68

ton, Illinois who owned a dry-goods store and was rich. My father took us to Alton to visit her before she died. My great-grandmother lived in a big white house with a porch all around it. There was a peach tree in the back yard, full of pink and green peaches. She gave us peach pie to eat with real cream, not ice cream, on top. By that time she was a very old lady. She had bookcases with glass doors and she opened one and gave Richard a copy of the Bible she had won in Sunday School for an attendance prize. She gave me a book of myths. It is on my bookshelf now. It has her handwriting in the front:

Adelaide Crawford
Toledo, Ohio
1890
"My book and heart
Shall never part."

She was very proud that my father had become a school principal.

She asked Richard and me if we were on a debating team. It turned out that she had been in the Ladies' Debate Society of her high school, and they had won a debate on "Resolved: That the United States, as a Great Power, Should Become Involved in the Affairs of the Orient," against a team from Springfield, Ohio. They went to Springfield by train for the debating contest. They stayed at the YWCA and had dinner at the best restaurant. She told us, "My, that was a good dinner! Didn't we just eat, and never paid a cent because we were the guests." You could tell how important that trip was to my great-grandmother. I guess it was the only trip she ever took, except to move to Alton, Illinois.

It is funny to think of my great-grandparents and grandparents growing up in this same country that I am growing up in, but without cars and highways and pizza stands and TV. My mother says that when she was little, and went to visit her grandmother in Michigan, a small town was as quiet as the country, and people took drives just to see the scenery, or to buy fresh eggs at a farm on the edge of town. On those visits my mother would sit on her friend Agnes Schreiber's porch, which was all covered with morning-glory vines and play Monopoly, or go to Sunday School picnics on Taylor's Cliffs, or swim in Crescent Lake. I found some pictures of my mother in Michigan, with shorts on and a hairbow on top of her head. She looked like herself even then. And I can imagine how she must have been— like herself, only younger, younger than I am now.

Sometimes I wonder what kinds of things I will do with my family, if I have a family. It makes me feel strange to think that somewhere, maybe in another state, maybe even in some other country, there is some person growing up and going to school and looking at old photographs and maybe fighting with his sister, that I might someday meet and decide to get married to. I can't imagine it. I wonder if there will *be* families, when I am grown up. I always read those magazine articles about how The Family is changing, but they never explain what it is changing *to*. I am glad my own family has stayed the same, except that we grew up.

Anyway, I know that I want to live alone for some time when I am grown, before I decide whether to be in a family. I would have my own apartment or house, work in the day and fix what I like for my supper, go on bike trips, travel to California or to Australia—I could do anything. One thing I am sure of is, I will do a lot of things. I will not get stuck in just one kind of job all my life, or live in just one place.

By the end of that Saturday, I had most of the pictures sorted. We ate supper in the kitchen so I could leave the pictures in piles on the dining room table. After supper we looked at them.

"You know," Ma said, "It always makes me feel strange to look at old pictures, and to try to imagine how people were feeling then. Could they guess that we would be looking at them all these years later? Did they think they would look old-fashioned some day? I wonder how strange all the ordinary pictures of us will look to somebody else years from now?"

It was just what I had been thinking. Ma and I are very alike in some ways. I like that.

71

10

I WAS ALWAYS glad to have Miss Peretti's class on Mondays. It was a good way to start the week.

Miss Peretti's room is the best place at Jefferson. She has chairs arranged in a circle, but people can sit on the floor if they want to, on cushions. Miss Peretti's room has yellow curtains at the windows, so the room turns gold when the sun shines. There are posters on the walls, and a bulletin board where you can put up a clipping from the paper or a picture you like or a poem you wrote or a notice about your lost cat if you have one. Miss Peretti cares about people's feelings.

I had three classes a week with her. Oliver was in my class, and Mary, and Arlene. When we were just starting at Jefferson that class really helped us to get adjusted. Miss Peretti says you can't work well with people unless you get to know them. The first day, she gave us crayons and cardboard and stars and ribbons and aluminum foil and kindergarten scissors, and we had to make name tags for ourselves. The whole first week, the topic was Who We Are. One thing we did was, each person interviewed a person they didn't know, and introduced that person to the whole class. I chose Arlene because I was a little bit scared of her because she is black, but I wanted to find out what she was like. I have begun to find out now, because Arlene is one of my best friends, but sometimes I think I will never really know her.

Arlene thinks about things and knows what she thinks and speaks her mind. I really want to be like her, tough and brave and strong-minded. Arlene reads Miss Peretti's *New York Times* every day, and she knows things like how many more blacks than whites go to jail because they can't raise money for bail, and facts like that. Arlene says people in Plainview County don't want apartments to be built here, even though we need apartments, because they are afraid more blacks will come here to live then. I told my mother what Arlene said, and Ma said Arlene is probably right. My mother wants to write an article about how Plainview County discriminates against blacks and poor people.

I'm really glad to have a friend who is black but I know enough by now not to say that to Arlene, because either she would get her feelings hurt, or she would laugh at me. I can never be sure which she'll do.

While we were getting to know each other, Miss

Peretti gave us essays to read. We read essays by James Thurber and Henry David Thoreau and Virginia Woolf and Russell Baker. Then we had to write essays ourselves. Sometimes Miss Peretti made up the subjects and sometimes we did.

That class was the place where I felt the most at home at Jefferson. Everybody in the class liked each other. I don't mean we were all good friends outside of class, just that we knew each other in a real way, because we talked with each other about things that were important.

So when Miss Peretti gave us an essay assignment called "I Wish," I tried to tell my real feelings about what was going on in my life: not just the facts about the petitions and the recommendations, but how I felt about them.

We had to read the essays out loud to each other. Some people wrote about peace: "I Wish There Would Be Peace Forever." Bobby Higham wrote "I Wish I Had a Corvette Sting Ray" and Miss Peretti said that was a perfectly reasonable wish and, in fact, she wished she had a Corvette Sting Ray herself. She never lets us laugh at things, or think we are better or more liberal than somebody else. Oliver wrote "I Wish Factories Were Fined for Polluting." Arlene wrote "I Wish I Were Not the Only Black in this Class."

We discussed each essay. It's really interesting to discuss things with Miss Peretti, because we don't have to raise our hands, or talk just to the teacher. We talk to each other, like normal human beings.

Arlene's essay really made me think. She said things she's never even said to me in private, like how lonely she feels sometimes, and other times she wonders if people are being nice to her because they think they ought to be nice to black people. Arlene is such a good writer!

Everybody was quiet after she read her essay. It was like serious work, thinking hard about other people's ideas.

Mary said, "I like to be with you because you are Arlene, and because you are so strong and smart. And I think being black is a strong, important part of who you are."

Arlene smiled a real smile at that.

I felt funny reading my essay after Arlene's. My problems seemed kind of cheap compared to hers. But they were real to me.

This is my essay:

<u>I WISH PEOPLE DID NOT TREAT ME</u>
<u>LIKE SOME KIND OF NUT</u>

I think people should say what they believe, and do what they say, and stick up for what they think is right.
But several times recently when I have tried to do this, people have either laughed at me or got angry at me or acted as though I was a nut, or called me one. After a

while, I begin to wonder: <u>am</u> I some kind of a nut? Or not?

I really think I am not. I am an ordinary, medium kind of person. I get along with people, do OK in school. The last thing I want is to be conspicuous. I hate to be conspicuous for any reason. I get embarrassed very easily, like if my mother talks too loud in the supermarket, or if my father makes too many jokes in the post office, or if I have to do something in front of people, like make an announcement in assembly. Sometimes I wish deeply that I could just go around doing things without anyone even noticing me. I have often thought how relaxing it would be to be invisible, like someone in a fairy tale.

But instead, I have made myself conspicuous by talking about equal rights for girls because I believe in equality. This is a serious question, not a joke. But when I have tried to make people understand, some people have laughed at me or called me a nut.

It is bad enough to be treated unfairly, but it makes me furious to be called a nut when you try to do something about it.

I am not a nut.

Nobody in Miss Peretti's class called me a nut or laughed at me, but nobody called me very smart, either.

Bobby Higham said, "It sounds as though you want to have everything your own way. Like you want people to bow down and salute you and say how wonderful your ideas are."

Arlene said, "There's no way, just no way, you can stand up for things and be invisible all at the same time. If you're going to say what you think, some people are going to get mad or laugh at you."

It was almost time for the bell to ring. I felt like apologizing to people for writing such a complaining essay.

Then Miss Peretti said, "I've been called a nut myself, so I know how it feels. I really could understand your feelings in that essay, Barbara. I might have written it myself, but not at your age. At your age I wasn't able to speak up the way you do."

She always says something nice to everybody.

Then she said, "I have to agree with Bobby, that you are expecting too much if you think people should agree with you right away. Everybody who stands up for her opinion is going to be called a nut by somebody else, you can count on that. But the only way to make any changes happen is to stand up and say what you think, and do something about it. Look at Rosa Parks. You do know about her?"

Arlene smiled and said Yes. I said Yes too, because my father told me about her. Everybody else said no.

Miss Peretti asked Arlene to tell about Rosa Parks, quickly.

Arlene said, "She was this black woman who sewed clothes in Montgomery, Alabama. One day when she was really tired after work she got on a bus, and sat down in the back, in the colored section. You had to sit in the back if you were colored, then. And then a lot of white people got on, and the bus driver said 'You coloreds stand up and give these white folks your seats.'

"And Rosa Parks said, 'Not me. I paid the same as anyone on this bus, and I'm not getting up.'

"So the bus driver called the police," Arlene went on, "and the police came and dragged Rosa Parks off the bus and arrested her."

Everyone said, "That's terrible!" and "That's not fair!"

"A lot of things were not fair then," Arlene said, "like drinking fountains that said WHITE or COLORED. You had to go to the right one to get a drink. Toilets the same. And schools."

The bell rang. Nobody moved.

"But that was the start of the civil rights movement, because the black people of Montgomery said that if Rosa Parks was arrested for staying in a bus seat she paid money for the same as everybody else, nobody was going to ride the buses any more. And they didn't. For months they never got on a bus. They made car pools, and they walked. And the bus companies went out of business. And Rosa Parks' case went all the way to the Supreme Court, and the court said you could sit on any seat on a bus if you paid for it, north *or* south. And that was the start of the civil rights movement, and that movement is still going on."

"Was Rosa Parks a nut?" Miss Peretti smiled at me.

We were all collecting our books and getting ready to go out.

"I still don't like to be called a nut," I said.

"Of course not," said Miss Peretti. "But you'd better get used to it if you're going to keep on speaking your mind."

"I guess so," I said.

"Now I wonder," she went on, "whether you'd give me a copy of your PE petition to read. I might want to take it to our next faculty meeting, and ask the PE staff to discuss it with the rest of us. After all, we need to rethink a lot of things that go on in school. I think it's time for some changes."

I smiled at that. "You must be some kind of a nut," I said.

ESSAY

ON RIDING A BICYCLE

I love my bike.

It is an old one, red, a three-speed racer from Sears. It has a saddle seat, a basket, hand brakes, and a license plate that says BARBARA NEW YORK that my father bought me when I got the bike two years ago.

The best thing about my bike is that it makes me free. With my bike, I can go anywhere: visit any friend I want, go to the library or to the store. Or, I can just ride without going any particular place. If I wanted to, I could ride all the way across the country on my bike. Of course in reality my parents would not let me, but the idea is true. Some day when I am older I intend to do it, with a friend and a saddle pack.

I love to ride my bike on a cool sunny day with the wind in my face. I like the way hard pushes make the bike spurt uphill, and I love how it feels to let go and swoop downhill. When I am riding my bike, I feel that I am in charge of all my time. If I want to go fast, I go fast. If I want to laze along and look at all the little weeds and weed shadows at the side of the road, I do that.

When you're riding along on a bike and other people come riding toward you, you feel friendly. They smile, you smile back. It's as though you know something about each other, which you do: you know how good it feels to be riding. People in cars are not always so friendly. Sometimes they come up behind you and honk suddenly and yell out their window at you. This is mean, not just because it scares you but also because you don't feel private and alone any more.

The worst thing that ever happened to me on a bike was when I caught my front tire in a sewer grating. At the time, I didn't know what had happened. I just knew that I was suddenly falling, very slowly, over my handlebars, and then there was this enormous crack and hurt, and I was lying on the street watching my bike turn over in the air and land on top of me. I thought I was probably almost dead. The man from the Sunoco gas station ran out and helped me sit up and said I could call my mother on his phone, but when I was up I could tell I was OK, except that my head and my arm hurt. So I just sat on the curb and rested and after a while I rode home. When I got home I started to shake, and then I cried and cried and my mother made me lie on the couch all afternoon. I had a big bump on my head and a bruise on my arm that turned blue, then green, then a disgusting yellow.

The best thing with my bike is something that happens nearly every day: I am riding along Washington Street toward my house in the cool afternoon air. The sun is low and

the maples are all lit up gold with sun-
light. I am watching the sky turn purple on
one side of me and orange on the other, and
thinking about what there will be for supper. The wheels of my bike make a little
crunching sound on the gravel. My legs are
tired from pumping. Then I make an easy
turn into my street, and coast softly all
the way to my house.

I pedal down the driveway past the yellow
kitchen light and get off and push my bike
into its place in the shed and close the
shed door. My legs still feel as though
they're working the pedals, and my hands
still tingle from holding the hand grips,
and I'm hungry, and I'm home.

11

THE NEXT PERSON who got called a nut was my mother.

By this time she had written a few by-line articles for the *Journal*. The first one was about a fashion show at the Thursday Afternoon Club. Ma's name was in black type: BY MARIAN FISHER. We went out to the Dairy Queen to celebrate with thirty-five cent sundaes.

Ma said, "I'll feel better when my name goes on an interesting article about housing or schools."

Richard said, "Or, Boy Genius Scores Ten Baskets!"

I said, "Girl, 11, Gets Paper Route."

Dad suggested, "Fisher Children Make Own Beds."

Ma's next article was about a little lamb that a family in Northview was raising from a bottle. Ma said she liked interviewing people, and writing a story fast for a deadline. But she wasn't crazy about that lamb. She said he was sort of mangy.

After that, there was another fashion show article—this one a his and hers pants show, with poems for all the models. One of the poems said:

Pat and Paul together make many scenes
In classes and parties in their striped jeans.

How can people write things like that! Ma said she was afraid someone would see her by-line and think *she* wrote the poems.

All her articles were printed in the "Food and Family" section of the paper. But she said, "I'm heading for the front page. Wait and see. Before the year is over."

Meanwhile, I was delivering papers every day as though I really had the route. Ma had taken my recommendations to the circulation manager. She says she told him: "This is about Barbara Fisher, my daughter. But I'm not asking you to change your rules because she's my daughter. I'm asking you to change them because they are discriminatory and *wrong*."

I bet she really made an impression on him. I know I couldn't talk like that.

But all the circulation manager said was, "I'm sorry, Marian, but a rule's a rule. Tell your little girl not to take it personally."

When she told me, I said, "But I *do* take it personally."

"Of course," said Ma. "That's the only way to take something important. Then, either you care enough to do something about it, or you let it go."

I told her I would not let it go.

Meanwhile, I was determined to prove how well I could do the paper route.

It wasn't winter yet, but a couple of times I had to deliver papers in the pouring rain. I had an old plastic drop-cloth that covered them up pretty well, except that it kept blowing up in the wind and blocking my view. On rainy days I got off my bike and took the papers right up to people's doors, so they wouldn't get wet. I was trying to be as conscientious as possible.

The chow dog began to know me, I guess, because sometimes he wagged his tail a little bit while he was barking and slobbering at me. What a revolting animal!

When I had finished the route, I would ride home, feeling nice and light with nothing in my bike basket. Then I would go in and set the table for supper.

Ma and Dad usually came home in the car together, unless Ma had to stay late. Then she got a ride with someone from the paper. The night Ma's big article came out was her late night. Dad and Richard and I were already eating. She came in, opened up the *Journal* and set it down right over our plates.

"Look!" she said. "I made it."

It wasn't on the front page, but on the editorial page where opinion articles go. It was a three-column article with a thick black by-line.

"I didn't write the headline," Ma said. "Mr. Pollachek did. He has very good news sense."

WOMEN'S ACTIVITIES NEED LIBERATION, WRITER SAYS

By Marian Fisher

Are fashion shows the only entertainment women in Plainview County want?

In this writer's experience, fashion shows make up more than half the schedule of women's organization events. During the past week, a fashion show was scheduled each weekday afternoon, and on Tuesday and Wednesday evenings as well. There was a hat show and a sportswear show, an evening dress show and a shoe show, and even a fashion show for dogs.

No one would suggest that a lighthearted social occasion to benefit a worthy cause is out of place. But perhaps it is time to ask some questions:

—Are clothes, and fashion shows, so important that weeks of afternoons should be devoted to them?

—Are there worthy local causes that could benefit more from volunteer help than from financial donations?

This writer contacted several local agencies to determine volunteer needs. Each one described urgent demands for volunteers.

At the County Home for the Aged, Mr. James Drake reported, "We need many kinds of volunteers, especially drivers to take people from this home to stores and outside events. We urge people to contact us."

Calls to Springfield Hospital, the Association for the Retarded, and other agencies raised more requests for help. At the hospital, Miss Alice Houghton said, "I wish we could show women our problems, the way the stores show them their clothes."

Perhaps Plainview County needs a Volunteer Switchboard to organize volunteer work. In any case, it seems clear that fashion shows and luncheons do little to solve the real problems that exist here, either for the less well-off or for the women who attend the fashion shows and wear the clothes.

"I wonder whether anyone will notice," Ma said. She did not have to wait long to find out.

The day after her article came out, the phone at the *Journal* rang all day with calls for her. Ma said a few people, like the woman she had talked to at the hospital, called to say thanks. But the rest of the calls were complaints. Mr. Pollachek took some of the calls, and asked people to write letters. He said he would print a special page of letters about Ma's article.

Dad said that a couple of women even called him at school to complain about what Ma had written.

"I told them that I had no control over my wife's opinions," he said, "but that, as a matter of fact, I agreed with her completely. I also suggested that Washington School could use some volunteer reading tutors!"

When we were upstairs, Richard came to my door and said, "A couple of people came up to me in school and said 'Hey, Fisher, your mother's going to get it.'"

"What did they mean?" I asked.

"Maybe their parents are writing mean letters to the paper," Richard said.

"What if all the letters are against Ma?" I asked.

"She'd still be right," Richard said.

"But it would be so awful for Ma to have to read pages of mean letters," I said. What I was really thinking was that it would be so awful for me to go to school and have people say, "I read those letters to your mother in the paper, ha, ha." The whole problem of being conspicuous was rising up again. I felt just a little bit sorry to be Marian Fisher's daughter, and I felt awful to feel like that.

Before I went to bed, I went downstairs and asked Ma, "Do you mind, about the phone calls, and the letters you'll get?"

Ma said, "Yes, it bothers me some. I feel a bit nervous and almost guilty, as though I'd done something wrong. But you know, I'm glad I wrote that article. So I'll just have to take what comes."

Then she kissed me and said, "Sleep tight, no bedbugs," which is short for Good night, sleep tight, don't let the bedbugs bite. Richard and I always used to say that before we went to bed.

When the letters about Ma's article were printed, they took up two full pages in the *Journal*. The headline said: FASHION SHOWS? OUR READERS RESPOND. There were seven letters *for* Ma, and sixteen against.

Here is an example of a good letter:

To the Editor:
I was pleased to read Marian Fisher's thoughtful analysis of women's activities in your paper. As a volunteer worker for the Mental Health Association, I know how important such work is. As a woman who is often asked to buy fashion show tickets, I can tell you how much I dislike them. I believe, along with Marian Fisher, that it is time for some changes in Plainview County. I think that she will help to bring about such changes with good articles like this one. Congratulations for printing it.

Jane Stillman
Fair Park

Here is just one example of a bad letter:

To the Editor:
Concerning the article by Marian Fisher about fashion shows, I have never read a more disgust-

ing piece of drivel! It appears that she has nothing better to do than drive around Plainview County criticizing our charitable work. Perhaps if she stayed home with her family and took care of them, she would be more content with herself and would not need to write such ridiculous articles.

Mrs. L. Raymond
Fair Park

You can imagine how I felt, reading letters like that about my mother.

Ma didn't seem to mind. She said, "Oh, well, it makes for an interesting paper." But I minded. I hated to go to school the next day and have people ask me, "Hey, did you see those letters about your mother?" and so on.

The first person I saw the next day was Oliver, who met Richard and me on the way to the bus stop. "What did your mother think about those letters?" he asked.

Richard said, "She said it was about what she expected."

"My parents think your mother is right," Oliver said. "They say someone should have written what she did a long time ago. My mother says she will never go to another fashion show, because she always hated them and now she's going to say so out loud."

That was a surprise. I really hadn't thought that

a newspaper article could actually make somebody change what they did.

People kept stopping me in the hall at Jefferson to say, "Hey, Fisher, I read those letters about your mother," or "Hey, Barbara, I saw your mother's name in the *Journal*." I didn't know what to say back.

I was glad I had Miss Peretti that day. I knew no one in that class would laugh at me or make fun of my mother.

I met Arlene going in. "Your mother sure is something!" Arlene said. "I wish I could write like her and make people mad and get them to think."

Mary said, "My mother says she admires your mother so much! She says your mother said what every woman in Plainview County thinks, but nobody else had the nerve."

Bobby Higham asked me, "Were your mother's feelings hurt?"

"Well, I guess so," I said, thinking about it. "But she said controversy makes an interesting paper. And she really believes what she wrote."

"I'm sure she does," Miss Peretti said. "Please tell your mother I read her article and I liked it very much. Now I know where you get your spunk."

"That's what I was thinking," Mary said. "Barbara *is* like her mother. She speaks her mind and she stands up for what she believes."

Miss Peretti said, "I think I should get a subscription to the *Journal* for this class, now that it's getting so interesting. Newspaper articles like Marian Fisher's are a kind of essay, really."

"Letters to the editor are like mini-essays," Oliver said.

"That's true, Oliver," said Miss Peretti. "You know, I never thought of that. That's a good point."

And we got off onto a discussion of journalism, and the influence of newspapers in people's lives. But I didn't talk much. I was saving up all the good things people had said, to tell my mother. I was really proud of her.

12

THAT WAS THE end of being inconspicuous for my mother, and the start of being famous. Richard became famous soon after—he scored three baskets in the first basketball game. Ma and Dad and I saw him do it. Everybody yelled, "Yea, Fisher!" and things. We were really proud.

And right after that I became very conspicuous myself. The way it happened was this. Miss Peretti told me that the faculty had spent a whole afternoon talking about "sex discrimination at Jefferson." And they decided to have an assembly on that topic. She wanted me to talk at the assembly!

All that week I worried about what I would say. I practiced speeches while I rode my bike along the paper route. I told the chow dog, "The time has come to end centuries of discrimination against women."

I told my family at supper, "Old ways must change. The day of women's liberation has arrived."

Dad said, "Barbara, I think you'll do better if you

93

keep your speech more personal, and just tell how you feel about things that happen to *you*."

That was very helpful advice.

The day before the assembly, there was a package for me on the mailbox when I came home from school. It was from Macy's. I couldn't guess why they sent me something.

I went inside, went to the bathroom, mixed up some orange juice, poured it, peeled a banana—just making myself wait to see what could be in the package. Then I sat down and began to open it. There was a dress inside, the prettiest dress I ever had in my life, yellow with blue and red flowers and silver buttons down the front. Ruffles on the cuffs. There wasn't any card in the box to say who it was from, but I knew it wasn't a mistake. It was just the kind of dress I like, and whoever sent it had to know me.

I was glad nobody was home. I hate to have somebody standing around when I try things on. I put the dress on in front of the upstairs mirror, and looked at myself, and I thought I looked good. The skirt had two pockets. I love pockets because I always have something to put in them—money, gum, a pencil, my hands. If I don't have anywhere to put my hands, I feel lost.

Some people say that if you are for women's liberation, then you shouldn't care about how you look. But I think that is crazy. I certainly do not want to have to spend hours and hours trying to look beautiful like some dumb fashion model, with false eyelashes and layers of make-up and a wig. But how I look is part of me, just like what I think or what I say or the things I do, and I like to feel good about myself. So I was glad to have that new dress.

That night Ma said she had ordered it for me. She saw an ad in the paper, and called up and asked Macy's to send it as fast as possible. "I thought you should have something special to wear for the assembly," she said. That was so nice of her!

Then it was assembly day. I woke up and remembered, and felt sort of scared. Then I remembered my new dress. I felt good when I put it on, almost the way I used to feel when I was little and got a new pair of red sneakers. I like that new clothes feeling.

My family wished me good luck. "Give 'em hell," my Dad said. "You certainly look pretty in that dress."

"I know you're going to be a very good speaker," said Ma.

Richard and I walked to the bus stop together.

"I'm sort of scared," I told him.

Richard said, "I'll be proud of you."

Assembly was first period. When I got to school I went right up on the stage. There were four of us: me, Miss Peretti, who was going to be the moderator, a teacher called Miss Ogden from PE, and Mr. Barnes, who is a shop teacher.

"You look pretty, Barbara," Miss Peretti said. "Are you nervous?"

I had to think about it. I realized that I was excited, but for some reason I didn't feel scared any more. We sat down on chairs on the stage and watched people come in. I saw Oliver. He waved at me. I saw Arlene. And lots of people I didn't know. The auditorium looks different when you are on stage looking out, instead of in the audience looking up.

Miss Ogden talked first. She told about how the PE teachers made up the PE course list. She said it depends partly on how many teachers there are who can teach the different sports. She said the school was going to hire another teacher in the next semester, and they would look for somebody who could teach tennis *and* modern dance.

She told about how sports are changing. "We used to emphasize competitive sports in schools," she said. "Now we're beginning to teach skills that everyone can enjoy, whether they are outstanding athletes or not. We have been thinking about starting co-ed volleyball, and opening our modern dance classes to boys."

Some people snickered at that.

Miss Ogden said, "I know that may seem strange to some of you. Some day, I hope it won't. After all," she pointed out, "you all dance, whether you're boys or girls."

I thought Miss Ogden was very reasonable. Maybe she had a hard time talking about her ideas with the older PE teachers. I knew Mrs. Bream wouldn't agree with them. But anyway, the PE teachers let her talk for them at assembly. That was a good sign.

Then Mr. Barnes talked about shop, and how he had wanted shop to be co-ed for years, but only one or two girls ever signed up. "Now," he said, "I think the times are right, and I am ready to invite every girl in this school to take shop for one semester."

There was a lot of cheering, some *boos*. I was thinking I would like to take shop, maybe next semester.

Then it was my turn. Miss Peretti introduced me as a girl who was working for equal rights. She told about the paper route, and how I was working to change the rule. I could tell some people didn't even know that girls weren't allowed to deliver papers. "All right," Miss Peretti said to me. "It's your turn, Barbara."

"I've been learning a lot of things about fairness and equality for girls," I said, and then I just began to tell about the things that had been happening to me. I was surprised to find how easy it was, once I had started. The whole auditorium was looking at me. I had the feeling people were really interested in what I was saying. It was amazing. I told about the slimnastics petition, and I said how dumb we had been to think everybody should agree with us.

97

"I don't mean we should cut out slimnastics," I said. "Some people really like it. I just mean that people who don't want to take slimnastics should be able to take other things. And there is no earthly reason why girls in this school should not get tennis lessons," I ended.

People clapped!

Miss Peretti asked for discussion. Some kids acted foolish, like one boy who said, "Let's see Barbara Fisher try out for the football team, ha, ha." A girl said she would never take shop because she was afraid she'd hurt herself with a hammer or something.

"That's why you should take it," Mr. Barnes said, "to learn to use tools safely."

After about fifteen minutes, the assembly was over. Miss Ogden said she would like me to come and talk at the next PE staff meeting. Miss Peretti said I had spoken very well. Mr. Barnes said he hoped I would come to his shop class next semester. Then I walked down the stage steps into the auditorium aisle, and a whole lot of people came to stand around me.

People said, "Hey, Barbara, you were good," and "Barbara, what about home ec?" and so on. Irene Norton, the girl who signed the PE petition, came over and gave me a pat on the shoulder.

When I was walking out, people called "Congratulations, Fisher!" Not one single person called me a nut, although I suppose some people might have thought I was one, privately. But I didn't care if some people disagreed. I had said what I wanted to say, in front of the whole school, without even feeling scared. I felt wonderful!

<u>ESSAY</u>

ON DOGS AS COMPARED TO PEOPLE

1. Dogs are direct and true. They tell
you exactly how they feel, whether they are
happy or miserable or sick. They don't try
to hide their feelings, or say "that's
wonderful" if it isn't wonderful. If a dog
doesn't like the food you put down, it just
doesn't eat.
2. Dogs are loyal. If you are kind to
them, and they are your dog, they love you.
They don't ask you to be popular or smart,
or any special age, race, or religion, or
fat or thin. It's all the same to a dog.
If it loves you, it loves you. You don't
have to wash your face and comb your hair
for it.
3. Dogs are grateful. Do any nice little
thing for a dog, like tell it "good dog,
good dog" and scratch it behind the ears,
and it acts as though you have performed
some major act of kindness—wiggles all
over, rolls around on the ground in happi-
ness. Give a dog a soup bone, even if you
didn't pay for it yourself, and the dog
will throw a fit of gratitude. Just say
the dog's name, and its tail will thump and
thump with pleasure.
4. Dogs don't hold grudges. You could

forget to feed your dog, or not let it come
along with you some place, or even yell at
the dog when it hasn't done anything to
you. But that dog will just keep on loving
you. It doesn't add up your mistakes and
hold them against you. It knows the way
you really want to be.
  5. Dogs are cozy. It feels so good to
lie on a rug next to a big dog and put your
head on its back and stroke its fur slowly.
Or to have a little puppy curled up in your
lap while you pat the soft hair around that
little pink stomach. On a cold night it is
warm and comforting to have a dog circle
around at the bottom of your bed and settle
down in a soft thumping weight on your feet.

  People are nice too. Their stomachs
aren't as cute as dogs' and they can be a
whole lot meaner. But I would rather talk
to a person than a dog, and when all is
said and done, in spite of arguments and
grudges, I love people like my mother and
father and brother much better than I could
possibly love any dog. Now that I am at
the end of this essay, I see that its theme
is the same old one about Different Things
Are Different. Dogs and people aren't in
a contest. Dogs are good for some things,
people for others.
  I still wish I could have a dog.

13

THE NEXT DAY I was just unlocking the front door when the phone began to ring. It was Ma.

"Guess what!" she cried. (I always hate that word in books, but that's really what Ma did—she cried out in a very excited tone of voice.) "Guess what the governor just did!?"

I couldn't imagine anything the governor would do that Ma would call up to tell me.

"He signed a bill that lets girls deliver newspapers!" Ma said.

"But what about my recommendations?" I asked. "What about all the work I'm doing to get the route? How come the governor just signs something and that's it?"

I felt confused. Of course, I was glad to know that the law was changed so it wouldn't be illegal any more for girls to deliver newspapers. But it seemed so unfair that nobody had paid any attention to me and the hard work I was doing by myself. Now the governor would get all the honor—and he wasn't even a girl. All he had to do was pick up his pen and sign a piece of paper. But I had been riding up and down the streets in the cold wind, making my way among cruel dogs and unkind humans who thought I was a nut, and nobody seemed to care.

I think Ma understood how angry and sorry for myself I felt.

She said, "You must be feeling sort of cheated. It *is* maddening to have other people get credit for something you worked for. But look at it this way: your point is made. And it's law. That's a real victory."

That was true. Now people would have to get their papers delivered by me, whether they wanted to or not! Ha, ha on them. I began to realize that, no matter how it had happened, I had won.

"I won!" I said. "Can I just go and have the route, then?"

"Well," Ma said, "Yes. No. Not exactly. You see, what the paper wants to do is sort of make a ceremony. They wanted a picture of you with the circulation manager—"

"I will not have my picture taken with that rude, unfair man!" I shouted. "I will *not!*"

"Barbara, I've already told them that," Ma said. "I was sure you wouldn't want a ceremony up here."

"They ought to come to me," I said, "and apologize."

"What I suggested," said Ma, "is for a staff photographer to come home with me tomorow, and take a picture of you on your bike. And Mr. Pollachek said fine. He says it will be a nice twist for me to write the story. So I'm calling to find out if that's OK with you, and if you'll come home promptly after school tomorrow."

"Sure," I said.

I was thinking that everybody on the block, and the whole paper route, and in my school, would read about me. I decided to wash my hair, so I would look nice in the picture.

"Barbara," Ma said. "One thing—would you mind washing your hair so you'll look good in the picture?"

"Oh, Ma, I was *going* to," I said. I wonder how old I will be before my parents stop telling me things to do, when I am already planning to do them.

Ma said, "If the governor knew about you, I'm sure he would be extra pleased about signing the bill."

That night Richard and Dad congratulated me about getting the route, and becoming a wage earner.

"A *legal* wage earner," Dad said.

"Always remember who gave you your start," said Richard.

"I thought that was your mother and me," Dad said.

"You merely produced the infant," said Richard. "I guided her through the highways and byways of newspaper delivery."

"And the governor was like a fairy godmother, giving his blessing with a fountain pen instead of a wand," Ma said.

I said, "I knew I was right, all the time."

Dad said, "You were. And that's an important thing to be. Now you can prove it by being reliable with the papers."

To myself, I pledged right then that I would be. I pledged I would deliver the papers as well or better than any deliverer ever had, even Richard.

14

WHEN OLIVER AND I got off the bus the next day we could see the *Journal's* station wagon parked in front of my house. It was nice to know that Ma was home waiting for me—the first time since school began.

Oliver said, "See you in the paper," and turned up his walk. I pushed open our front door. There was Ma having coffee in the living room with the photographer, a young man with a beard. He had a camera bag over his shoulder. He got up from the couch and came over to me to shake hands.

"This is Jim Burns, Barbara," my mother said. "Jim, this is my daughter Barbara." I could tell my mother was proud to introduce me.

"I'm really glad to meet you, Barbara," Jim Burns said. "I told your mother, I think it's wonderful that you stood your ground with the *Journal*. Too bad the governor stepped in before you won out on your own. I know you would have."

"Did you ever meet the circulation manager?" I asked. "I'm not so sure."

"Oh, there's always somebody like him," Jim Burns said. "Where my girlfriend works, in a gas station, there's one man who always heckles her. She doesn't care. She knows the customers keep asking for her because she's a good mechanic. Times are changing, Barbara. You're part of it."

That was a new idea to me, that I was part of changing times. "Then so's Ma," I said. "She's working to change things, too."

"Right," Jim Burns said.

Ma laughed. "Oh, I don't know," she said.

"You are," said Jim Burns. "The *Journal*'s really been different since you came on. I have a feeling you're going to shake up the whole county before you're through."

"Let's go shake up Maple Street a bit and get our photos," Ma said. "I have to get back and write up Barbara's story before six tonight."

"Why don't you just load up the papers on your bike and start off, and I'll take your picture as you go along," Jim said. I went upstairs and changed into my jeans and my best shirt and brushed my hair hard. Then I went to the shed, pulled out my bike, loaded the papers in the basket and started off, slowly, with Jim Burns and Ma following me. It was amazing how easily I could balance my bike with all the papers in it, even when I was riding so slowly. I had learned a lot since I began the route.

At the Warners' the door opened and all the boys came out at once.

"Barbara!"

"Hey Barbara!"

Then one of them saw Jim and my mother.

"Hey, Barbara, you getting your picture taken?"

"Barbara, Barbara, take my picture?"

They all came crowding around. Jim took a couple of pictures.

"Hey, mister, take my picture too?"

"Look at me, I can stand on my head!"

Mrs. Warner came to the door. "What's going on?" she asked.

"The governor signed a bill to let girls deliver papers," I yelled to her. "I'm getting my picture taken for the *Journal*."

"Oh, that's lovely, Barbara," Mrs. Warner called. "You certainly deserve it."

Lorraine and Laverne came next.

"Barbara, Barbara!"

"How come you're getting your picture taken?"

"Hey, take my picture?"

"Mine!"

Mrs. Baskin came out. "Hello, Barbara. Hi, Mrs. Fisher. What's going on?"

So we told her. "That's wonderful!" she said. "I'm so proud of you, Barbara. You're a real pioneer."

"Barbara isn't a pioneer, Mommy," yelled Lorraine. "She doesn't have a spinning wheel or a churn." I could tell that the first grade at Park Street School was studying pioneer life, as usual.

Ma asked Mrs. Baskin if she could quote her recommendation of me in the news story. Mrs. Baskin said she would be honored.

"Hey, Barbara," Laverne called out. "You're going to baby-sit us tomorrow."

"I know it," I said. "See you then."

Ma said, "I think maybe it would be good to take a couple of shots on Spring Street where the houses are closer together."

They went back to the station wagon, and I rode on around the corner to Spring Street. Pretty soon I was into my stride, riding along and throwing the papers smooth and easy. When I came to the chow's house I heard the crunch of the station wagon slowing down behind me, and Ma saying to Jim, "OK, let's stop here."

I stopped my bike to wait for them before I threw the paper. Wouldn't you know that that dumb chow dog would come snuffling up the sidewalk drooling and yipping and wagging around with its fur all matted, jumping at me. I think it was trying to be my friend, I really do. I wish I could get over my prejudice about chow dogs, but it is so hard. I can't stand to watch that drool run out of their mouths and eyes.

Jim was taking pictures behind me. I said, "Go home, doggie, go home," and the chow calmed down and turned around and snuffled back to his door.

I got back on my bike and rode on down the street,

with Jim coming after me taking pictures. At the end of Spring he got in the station wagon and Ma pulled it up beside me.

"Thanks, Barbara," she said. "We got a lot of good shots. We have to get back now so I can write the article. I'll see you later. Remember, this is my late night."

"So long, Barbara," said Jim. "Congratulations!"

They drove off and I went on to finish the route. By this time I could do it almost as fast as Richard. I was getting to be a real pro.

15

THE NEXT DAY Ma burst into the house with ten copies of the *Journal.* "You're on the front page!" she said, smiling excitedly.

It was a good picture, I thought. Unfortunately, the chow was in it too, snuffling after me, spoiling the dignity of the whole thing. I guess that was really realism. The caption under the picture said:

Barbara Fisher, 11, of Fair Park, first Plainview County girl to deliver newspapers after the governor's signature ended discriminatory hiring, encounters a common paper route hazard as she rides down Spring Street.

The headline said:

PAPER ROUTE BILL SIGNED; LOCAL GIRL READY

By Marian Fisher

Barbara Fisher was a step ahead of the governor. On the day he signed a bill making it legal for girls to deliver papers, Barbara was already riding her route. Despite official discouragement and the prospect of breaking the law, Barbara took over her brother's paper route last month, and was mounting an independent campaign against discriminatory rulings. Barbara's mind was made up before the governor changed his. "After all," Barbara said, "it is fair for girls to have the same chance to work hard and earn money that boys have."

Some of Barbara's customers expressed pleasure that she was taking over the route. "Barbara is a regular baby sitter for my children," said Mrs. Ann Baskin of Maple Street. "She is reliable and prompt and I feel sure she will make an excellent delivery girl."

Other customers wondered whether Barbara would be as dependable as a boy. Barbara's brother, Richard, did not miss a day in two and a half years of delivering the *Journal,* until he turned the route over to Barbara a few weeks ago.

As for Barbara herself, she has no doubts. "I knew I could do the job," she says, "before the governor did. I am glad that he has decided that the girls of New York State are as dependable as the boys. I think my customers will learn the same thing. I plan to be a worthy replacement for my brother."

Barbara is the daughter of Marian and Alan Fisher, and lives with her family on Maple Street.

The *Journal* is proud to salute its new delivery girl, Ms. Barbara Fisher. James McGinnis, *Jour-*

nal circulation manager, says he welcomes paper route applications from other girls in the area.

That last sentence certainly did not tell the whole story. I knew a lot of the news behind this news, that's for sure.

You can imagine how good it felt to deliver the papers with my mother's story about me to everyone on my route. First of all, I stopped at Oliver's to show him.

"Hey, that's really good," Oliver said. "You have to autograph our paper, Barbara." He got me a pen, and I wrote YOURS TRULY, BARBARA FISHER across my picture. "Congratulations," Oliver said. "Now you're really famous."

I felt famous, riding along and delivering papers with my mother's news story about me right on the front page. I stopped at the Warners' and the Baskins' and showed the kids my picture.

"Hey, Barbara, you're in the *paper!*" said one of the Warners, as though I didn't know.

"Barbara's in the paper! Barbara's in the paper!" they all shouted.

"Hey, Barbara, you're famous!" said Lorraine.

"Barbara, will you still baby-sit us tomorrow?" Laverne asked, as though being in the paper would change what I would do.

"Of course," I told her. "See ya."

Then I went zooming around the turn into Spring Street, throwing papers in great high curves, and thinking about the good news I was tossing at people's houses.

The old chow came out, jumping and drooling.

"Hey, there," I told him. "Do you know you're famous? Your picture's in the paper." I decided to go and ring the chow dog's doorbell. Then I wished I hadn't. Then the man came out, and I told him.

"I thought you'd like to know your dog's picture's in the paper," I said.

"What's that?" he asked.

"Look," I showed him.

He began to read. Then he smiled. "Well, for goodness' sake," he said. "Isn't that something? So you're going to be a lady paper deliverer! And they took your picture with Sunny here. How about that, Sunny? Do you know you're in the news?"

What a name for that dog—Sunny! Anyway I was glad to know it, so I could calm him down by calling him by his right name.

"Well, so long," I said. "I've got to give out the rest of the papers."

"Keep up the good work," he called after me. As though he had thought it was good work before! Still, I was glad that he would be friendly from now on. It makes me feel better to deliver papers to friendly houses.

I finished the route in record time that night. Even so, when I came home it was nearly dark. The sky was that sort of twilight purple, with a few red streaks left over from the sunset, and it was turning cold. I realized I'd have to wear gloves soon. All the houses I passed on the way home looked cozy and warm with people moving inside yellow windows. At our house, the porch light was on.

And when I went inside, supper was all cooked, and the dining room table was set with our best tablecloth.

"Hello, Sweetie," Ma said. "Go and wash up. We're having a special meal tonight."

It was spaghetti and meatballs, my favorite. Richard loves it too. He said he was glad I had become famous.

"I think it's sex discrimination in reverse," he said. "Nobody put my picture in the paper when I started delivering papers."

Dad said, "I guess we'll just have to put up with the fact that the women in this family are getting famous."

"And Richard," I said.

"And you too, Richard," said Dad. "That leaves me the only un-famous one."

(That's not really true. Oliver's father, who is on the school board, told me once that my dad is famous for being the best principal in our district.)

That night, I put out my new dress, and a new pair of tights, to wear the next day. I decided that if I was going to be famous at school, I might as well look good.

16

I WAS FAMOUS! When I got on the school bus, people called, "Hey, Fisher! I saw your picture in the paper!" and so on.

At school, when I walked down the halls, everybody said, "Hey, Barbara, I saw you in the *Journal*."

In Miss Peretti's class, we discussed the anti-discrimination rule. At lunch time, my friends made me sign their newspapers. Irene Norton stopped me in the hall to say Congratulations.

It was a wonderful day. That afternoon, half the people on my paper route were waiting at the door to say Hello, or Congratulations. Old Sunny Chow Dog came snuffling up to me when I got to his house, and I patted him before he even jumped on me. He didn't seem to be drooling as much as usual. The man in the house came to the door to say "Congratulations, again," to me.

Sunny followed me back up the walk. "I really cannot stand chow dogs," I told him, "but for a chow dog you are not so bad." Sunny waggled and snuffled and drooled on my hand, and I told him "good doggie" before I realized what I had said.

It was really cold when I got back to Maple Street that night. Winter was getting closer. I knew my big challenge lay ahead, but I was ready for it. Through rain and storm and ice and snow and hail and sleet and everything, I would deliver the papers faithfully. I knew I could do it. I felt very sure of myself, and proud.

That night I went to baby-sit Lorraine and Laverne.

They kept talking about my picture in the paper.

"Barbara, we cut out your picture," Lorraine said.

"We hung it up on the bulletin board," Laverne said.

They showed me. It looked very official to see my picture and my mother's news story on somebody's bulletin board.

Before Lorraine and Laverne go to bed, I always read them a book. I like reading little kids' books, they're interesting. That night, they had a library book called *Things We Do*. It was about different kinds of work and play. I was reading along, when all of a sudden I realized that book was saying unfair things. One page said, "Boys like to climb trees and jump off high places." Then you turned the page and it said, "Girls like to play quietly with their dollies."

Lorraine and Laverne were getting sleepy. They were sort of dozing while I read to them. Then I came to this page that said, "Big boys deliver papers in the afternoons." There was a picture of a boy riding along as though he thought he was so great, and a girl was standing there with her hands behind her back, watching him.

Lorraine sort of woke up, and she said, "Hey, Barbara, that's a crazy book!"

Laverne said, "*Girls* deliver papers in the afternoon. Like you!"

I really felt proud when Lorraine and Laverne used me for an example. I realized that no matter what the books said, or no matter what the people on my paper route used to think, or no matter what the circulation manager at the *Journal* told me, and no matter what the governor used to think, I, Barbara Fisher, had stood up for my true feelings and now people were changing their minds. And even little kids could see that the times were changing.

Some day, when Lorraine and Laverne and other girls about six or so grow up to be free and be themselves and take what classes they want in PE, and become paper deliverers or mechanics or newspaper reporters or doctors or astronauts, partly it will be because of people like me who helped to change the times.

I am *not* a nut. I am a pioneer.

THE END

THERE REALLY ISN'T any end to this book, except that I have decided to stop. I keep on changing, and so do the people in my family, and my friends. Things that happen in the world change, and so do the days and the years.

I began writing about myself back at the beginning of sixth grade, when I was eleven. That seems an awfully long time ago now, when I am finishing sixth grade and have turned twelve. (I got a new bike for my birthday—a ten-speed Schwinn! I also got a saddle pack and a Youth Hostel membership. This summer Mary and Arlene and I are going on an overnight bike trip. Oliver will do my paper route for me when I am gone. Boys can deliver papers too, you know.)

I won't have a class with Miss Peretti next year, but she wants us all to stop in and visit her after school. She says she will use some of our class's essays for examples for the next class.

There is going to be co-ed tennis next year, and

also volleyball. Oliver and I have already signed up for tennis. I hope we'll be in the same class, but anyway we can play together after school.

Richard will be in high school next year. He will go on a different bus and everything. This summer he is going to be swimming counselor at the camp he goes to. He always writes me funny post cards, like a picture of the lake with an X in the middle and a balloon that says WISH YOU WERE HERE, GLUB, GLUB.

Ma and Dad say that it makes them feel grown up to see Richard and me growing. Ma says she is changing more than she used to think she would. "When I was a girl," she says, "I used to think everything just ended when you had a nice family. Now, I see that that's just the beginning." My father always says, "The only constant is change." I think I am beginning to understand that.

The best change that happened to me is that I got chosen to be Feature Editor of the Jefferson *Echo* for next year. The other editors chose me because Miss Peretti showed them my essays, and they liked my speech in assembly. I'm going to get people to write articles about their real feelings, like essays, for the *Echo*. I will not have articles about Popular Johnny Johnston, or gossip about who went to the Coffee Shop with who. I have already asked Arlene to write "Being Black at Jefferson" and she said she will. I'm going to ask one person in each grade to write "What's Good About Jefferson" and "What's Wrong With Jefferson." I think this will help to make the *Echo* be what it says on the masthead, "A voice of the students at Jefferson Middle School." It's going to be fun to work on the *Echo*. There is a real office, with desks and typewriters and baskets to put your articles in. We can work there after school every day.

I think the best thing about my life this year was my friends. There seem to be more interesting things to do with your friends when you grow up, and there are more people to be friends with. But also, I have spent a lot of time by myself this year. Just writing this book took hours and hours. In case you think it is easy to write about yourself, you should try it. You will see how complicated it is to explain things so that somebody else can understand what you are like. At the same time, writing is very enjoyable. When I say something just the way I want to say it, I feel really excited and good. I can see why people want to be writers.

Of course, in this book I have only told about part of my life. Some things are much too private to write about, and some are too silly. But I have tried to do what I said I would, and use realism and put down my true thoughts and feelings.

The worst thing about this year is the same as always. I did not get a dog. All the time I was writing, I kept hoping I could say "Dad came home last night with a wonderful surprise wrapped in a blanket," or "Ma made me close my eyes, and she led me out to the back shed, where a soft little whimper told me . . ." But this did not happen. So I will have to make my own happy ending: Some day, I will have a dog.

Betty Miles is the author of many popular books for children, among them *Just Think!, A House for Everyone, What is the World?, A Day of Autumn, A Day of Spring* and *Save the Earth!* Several of her picture books are now available as Pinwheel Books.

In addition to being a writer, Betty Miles is also a teacher at Bank Street College of Education and a frequent contributor to educational journals. This is her first novel for young people. She lives in Tappan, New York.